# Of All The Ways To Die

# Of All The Ways To Die

Brenda Niskala

QUATTRO BOOKS

**Canada Council
for the Arts**

**Conseil des Arts
du Canada**

*We acknowledge the support of the Canada Council for the Arts*
*which last year invested $20.1 million in writing and publishing throughout Canada.*

Cover art: Christpher Stanley Dubois (photograph by Available Light)
Author's photograph: Focus 91, photo by Larry Reynard
Cover design: Diane Mascherin
Text Typography: Grey Wolf Typography

Library and Archives Canada Cataloguing in Publication

Niskala, Brenda
    Of all the ways to die / Brenda Niskala.

ISBN 978-0-9810186-6-9

    I. Title.

PS8577.I75O3 2009          C813'.54          C2009-904951-1

Published by Quattro Books
P.O. Box 53031, Royal Orchard Postal Station
10 Royal Orchard Blvd., Thornhill, ON  L3T 3C0
www.quattrobooks.ca

Printed in Canada

*the living become ghosts when*
*their hearts wander off*

– John Livingstone Clark,
*Man Reading Woman Reading in Bath*

The headache hit, a heavy claw cramping the back of Urma's brain. She curled, fetal, and moaned, but had to stand, to stumble to the toilet, retching yesterday's meals, each lurching a cry as the knives in her brain skittered, nicking arteries, clogging blood flow, leaking into the space between the pia mater and the arachnoid membrane. Sub-arachnoid. Beneath the spider. Sweet blood. And then what?

Strange, the memories that last. The ambulance attendant cracking jokes, the emergency nurse's serious eyes and laughing mouth; the alarming jolt from gurney to bed, the peaking pain whenever Urma responds to the orientation questions, which are repeated every hour: *Do you know what your name is? Do you know where you are?* The tentative hovering smiles, the white and grey angles where hospital walls meet ceilings, the doctor telling her to breathe and not to worry. Worry about what? And these memories are lost: Urma's last week at work, the last time she talked with Eileen, the last thing that happened before the haemorrhage. Gone.

She is supposed to be opening the restaurant. She wants to be looking for Eileen, who is just a kid, after all. Instead Urma's brain is engaged in the tunnel of the MRI, the CAT scan and finally in an angiogram of her brain – the radioactive heat in the horseshoe of her skull a searing echo of the peaking pain; of the hole in her consciousness. She remembers the doctor's warning as they insert dye into the groin artery and watch it push up the carotid arteries, into the lovely webs of bloodflow throughout her brain: a slip of the needle could mean loss of sensation; a change in pressure could trigger the suspended aneurism. No one warned her of the incredible dizziness, the nausea – each lurching movement of the dye in her brain reactivating the headache. No one told her about the worst part of all – absolute stillness after the angio until the groin wound closes over, the process of diagnosis worse than the symptoms themselves.

Urma doesn't realize she is groaning. A nurse appears beside her, whispers, "Here, I'll give you something for that." The nurse's dark hand holds a needle which inserts a measure of fluid into the intravenous tubing.

"What's in that needle? No morphine, please!" Urma had already argued, ineffectively, it seems, about the logic of keeping her alert enough to answer their questions every hour, but stoned enough to make any response difficult. Urma did not like morphine. Or any drug, for that matter. Too many years working next door to the methadone clinic. Too many years of watching her friend Shannon numb herself to death. Urma had promised she'd be a guardian, keep on eye on Shannon's daughter, Eileen, and Eileen is missing.

"Morphine makes me nauseous," she lies. "Do you have anyone who can do massage?" That's what she needs most of all, to take the spasm out of her back. After the angio, her legs were strapped tightly to the bed so she can't roll anything but her head, which hurts like hell.

"You're to lie perfectly still until the doctor has a look at your incision." The artery where the dye was inserted could re-open, could flow freely, they had already told her. When was that? A day ago? Two days?

"When will the doctor see me?"

"Tomorrow morning, first thing." The nurse finishes inserting the morphine. "Try to get some rest."

Urma watches her leave, drowses a few moments, and opens her eyes to a nurse leaning over her. "What's your name? Where are you?"

"I know who I am and I know where I am. I want to get up and walk. I need to move. To get out of here. This is torture!"

The nurse's brown eyes grow wide. "Please just be still and answer the questions. Is there anything I can get you for your discomfort?"

"A walk and a massage. Please."

"You absolutely may not walk, and we do not have a massage therapist on the ward. Even if we did, you would not be able to have a massage at this time."

Urma knows that is reasonable. By the darkness in the ward, she sees it has to be the middle of the night. Her neck, her shoulders, her entire upper back is in spasm. She knows she needs help, human touch. "I have to move. Undo my leg straps, please."

"If you open that wound, you will bleed to death. Please sit still, Miss." The nurse pushes the help button by Urma's arm. Another nurse and an orderly swing into the space around her bed. The striped curtain rolls closed. They are checking charts, preparing another injection.

"Screw off! I have got to move. I will take all responsibility if I bleed to death or worse." Urma tears the intravenous tape and pulls the needle from her hand, worms her left leg free, arches her back, and slowly pushes herself up. Her head pounds, but that could be the drugs, being forced to lie absolutely still on her back for twenty hours after the angio, or the return of the headache. The heart rhythm in her ears.

The nurses and the orderly stand by expectantly, not touching her. Urma does not faint, her incision does not spurt blood, the sky does not fall in. From that moment on, Urma is on the fast track out of there.

A slow fast track: weeks. Twice doctors take her aside to assure her that she is lucky to be alive, that she is fortunate to have all her faculties. All the main ones, anyway. She could have had a stroke, like the woman across the way, who only nods when her husband lectures her, and weeps when her small children try to communicate with her. Urma could have had a tumour, like the woman in the next bed, wrapped like a mummy, eyes vacant, oddly innocent. The sixteen-year old girl who had the same kind of bleed as Urma has lost her sight. Urma could have lost much more than a few days of memory, a few weeks of work, and her self-confidence. In fact she has lost a lot more. She doesn't have time to be sick. She has a kid to find. Eileen might need her.

After two weeks of 'Please take it easy, Miss. You need rest to recover' it becomes clear to Urma there is no medical cure. Urma discharges herself.

Now, after three months of waiting for the headache to end, her blood vessels have apparently healed themselves. "God is great!" says the doctor, showing her the tangle of arteries captured on film. He points excitedly to where the carotids leading to her brain have adapted to the situation. Now she has to adapt. Live with the headache. Every massage therapist in the city has refused to touch her knotted neck and back. Too risky.

"You should not do anything to jar your head and neck," the doctor tells her.

"For now?"

"For ever."

"So car accidents are out of the question. Mosh pits and bungee jumping. Anything else?" She supposes sex is still possible. He's kind of cute, she decides, and maybe would know something about how to cure a headache.

"You could take an aspirin a day." He appears serious. It is the only tool they have, she knows, but surely not good for a bleed. Isn't that what they worried about when her father was under the knife? When he did not recover.

"I may need an aspirin or two tomorrow, because I'm throwing a party tonight!" Urma says. "Would you care to come?"

"How very kind." The good doctor pats Urma's shoulder lightly. "But I must decline. Socializing with patients is inappropriate, I'm afraid."

"But look, you're not my doctor anymore, right? There's nothing more you can do for me, right?"

"Perhaps another time." He smiles kindly.

Urma is disappointed but undaunted. "Another time, for sure." She has not had much male companionship for a long time. Well, ever since the injury, the haemorrhage. Really, who would want to get involved with a potential zombie? At least in his case, she wouldn't have to explain her lapses in memory, the bit of oddness she might show. Her swiss cheese brain. Besides, the way the invitation list was shaping up, he would be the only other living person there.

Urma wakes up from another night of trying to ease the headache, of trying to slow down the drumming anxiety of her new close relationship with death, of dreaming about the people she loves, so many of them gone, and Eileen still missing, and Urma settles on the idea of gathering everyone together who could possibly help her, those who could shed some light on where Eileen might be found. Those who could help her deal with her thudding sadness. As it turns out, most of them are not alive.

Urma decides to invite – no, it is more than a decision to invite – Urma invokes the dead to join her for supper that evening. Not dinner, you see, as that's something one has at noon if you're working hard with your body, and in the evening if you're not. Supper is something you do with friends, not so much to entertain as to commune. And it is to be a pot luck. For all she knows, a recipe exchange might be as close as the dead can get to really experiencing food, but Urma wants something from everyone, a few scraps of wisdom shared, if only from the margins of a recipe card. After fifteen years of serving coffee and burgers, she is ready to try some adventures with food too. What was it Eileen's kokum used to say? Live to eat and eat to live.

So Urma spends the next day preparing. She makes a list of the loved ones she'd like to see again. And a few people she'd like to meet. She leaves the list in the form of an invitation – her invocation – on the table, in the afternoon sunshine, in her neatest handwriting.

> *"It's a pot luck! Please come join me tonight at six*
> *for an evening of conversation. Feel free to bring*
> *a friend and your favourite food and recipe. Lots*
> *of love, Urma."*

Shannon tops the list of invitees. And of course that means Dwain too. And Dwain's muse – why not? A muse could bring the wisdom she yearns for. Eileen's kokum was wise, always. Tom, the legend from Urma's father's community, the closest Urma has to a muse, is invited. And Roger, who, like Shannon, checked out way too soon. Urma longs for his flippant insights, and he was a friend of Eileen's. St. Anthony, on the recommendation of Urma's friend, Princess. Can't hurt to have a saint along, especially one who is good at finding things. And Eileen. Just in case she is in a place where she can be invoked. Just in case she is dead.

Urma sets extra places for surprise guests, always a good strategy at a pot luck, and makes lots of her current favourite dishes – Thai chicken strawberry, vegetable yellow curry, chilli chocolate mousse. Heat, she thinks, that's what they will look for in a meal. And comfort. In order not to offend anyone, she replaces her stainless steel knives with plastic and turns her clocks and photographs to the wall, things she has read in some book or another would ease the spirits' minds.

She also spends a good amount of time cleaning and dusting, something she just hadn't felt up to for quite some time. Urma walks through her entire home breathing in the lemon, the pine, the cinnamon, the sweet cooking smells over cleaning vinegar.

At six her table is set and glows with the light of three new white candles. It is late fall, and the sun begins to weaken, filtering through the west and south windows, an outstanding harvest sunset just visible through the elms that still shade this part of the city. This is before they begin to curl their leaves and die, too, one by one, leaving gaping holes in the skyscape.

# THE CRAB APPLE INSIGHT

Eileen's mother, Shannon, was a poet. She also worked the streets – not great money, and there was always the danger of being ripped off, beaten, or worse, but at least Shannon was close to a place to shoot up, to a source of some yums. Her drug of choice was morphine, of course – you don't get much sweeter – but after she'd started The Change, the midlife crisis – as if she needed another crisis – business wasn't as good, and Talwin, Ritalin, whatever mix and match was available, would do. She had three doctors and a pharmacist as regular customers. But Shannon always shot up cautiously so she wouldn't get sick, because she was still on methadone. And she now drew the line at crack. That was for losers. It was because of crack cocaine that they took her baby Eileen away the first time. Fifteen years ago. Never again.

In early September of Shannon's last year alive, she had a poetic epiphany that summed up her life's work. Standing on her usual corner, underneath the shade and shelter of an ageing crab apple tree, she began to giggle to herself and ran to the nearby pay phone to call her confidant, the waitress from the restaurant next door to the methadone clinic, the one who would listen. Urma answered on the first ring, with a muffled "Mmallo?"

"Well hello there! It's Shannon."

"What's wrong, Shannon? Are you alright?" The last call had been weeks ago from a gas station out of town where Shannon had been turfed by a bad john, bruised and weeping.

"Oh, fine. Wonderful. I'm just out here picking crab apples."

"Are they good eating?"

"No, they're old and wrinkled and kind of sour tasting." Shannon's voice could make old and wrinkled sound sexy.

Urma knew the corner, knew the tree, and imagined Shannon standing at the payphone, one eye on the street, twirling a strand of her carefully combed black hair.

"Why don't you try the pincherries instead? They're just across the street."

"Those young ones haven't got the money, honey. Gotta go. Love you"

Gone before Urma could say good-bye.

Shannon's crab apple insight could have been a potent observation about The Fallen Poet finding Beauty in Squalor, and needing a Lifetime of Dying to Learn to Live. But Urma guessed Shannon hadn't wasted much time in introspection, had likely already eased herself into a well-polished car, having picked up a rather pickled crab apple that afternoon.

This is not how Shannon dies, however, and happens long before Urma's brain injury, before Shannon arrives decked out in turquoise at Urma's dining room table.

Like most of the people on the street, Shannon was an incurable romantic, looking for someone to love her and her alone. By sharing his lurid fascination with people and things long buried, and occasionally sharing with Shannon a snippet of poetry from the book by Shelley, Dwain left Shannon with the distinct impression that this was love. Finally, the real thing.

Dwain was good-hearted, but vain, as farm boys brought up in the plentiful years of the late '70s were. A fallen prince, Shannon and Urma said, brought up to believe the world was his oyster, and then, when the shell opened, finding there was no pearl inside. He could do the indignant 'Don't you city folks know where your food is coming from?' as well as any prairie person, and hated it when he got the usual answer: 'From Safeway'.

Dwain had to leave the farm after the Crow Rate was taken away, wheat prices bottomed to all-time lows, the Americans stopped buying Canadian beef, and even chickens were becoming a risky investment. No matter where they lived, people still needed water, and so Dwain dug trenches, dug wells, found water. He showed Shannon how to dowse.

"Here, Shannon, hold these." They were two copper rods, bent at right angles, parts from an old record album stand. "Keep your hands loose, like this." He wrapped his arms around her and placed his hands under hers. "Now walk, slowly, just walk around the lawn."

In a postage stamp of a yard, with crumbling saw-toothed fences on two sides, the unpainted back steps of her current home behind them and the gravel alley ahead, Shannon could swear she smelled peavine in his hair, sweetgrass on his skin. She took a few steps, leaning back into his chest. Suddenly the copper rods moved of their own accord, like a magnet pulling at them, pointing down. Shannon yelped and twirled to face him, flooded with images of springs and artesian wells emerging from the cracked ground.

"There," Dwain laughed. "You have just found the sewer line."

Dwain loved the earth. The scent of it after a rain, the feel of it, sun warmed in your hands, rich with potential. The sweet depths as he drilled through the sandy layers, the layers of yellow and red clay, the smooth texture of shale and the grit of the coarse gravel, all of them intrigued him with their secrets, their unexposed pasts.

He feared the earth too. Not the depths, but their exposure. Whenever he opened the earth's belly to the elements, the walls of the trench sodden and crumbly or slick, sliding back to hide what was opened for the first time to the sun, he felt the weight of the fall, the crushing power a thrill of fascinated apprehension in his guts, a tingling in his legs. With a welldigger's version of vertigo, he leaned over the pits and trenches, dizzy with morbid desire.

Dwain watched and read everything he could get his hands on about death by crushing, and, in an attempt to cure his fear, he adopted a bog mummy as his muse. He would entertain Shannon, and often Urma, with the details of speculation on how the bodies came to be buried in the acidic peat of northern England.

"I'm going to take you travelling," he'd tell Shannon, "and I'll show you all kinds of museums."

Dwain dreamed of the British Museum. For years he'd clipped everything he could about the Fox Man, the bog mummy housed there. The body crushed by the bog, tanned by the acidic peat moss, curled into a twist of limbs, a strip of fox fur on his arm. The face of the young man Fox Man must have been before the bog was tacked in postcard form on Dwain's fridge. They'd often commune first thing in the morning, especially after a bit of a bender.

"How you doing this morning, Fox Man? Me? I'm not doing so great. My head hurts. My whole body hurts, if you want to know the truth. I wish to hell I hadn't had that last pitcher of beer. But I'm still alive, and you aren't." That was, of course, while Dwain was really still alive.

"It's not right," was Urma's comment when Dwain was musing on his muse. She'd seen Fox Man in London, at the

British Museum, when she was much younger and had a traveller's spirit. "Putting bodies on display in museums like that. Doesn't the guy get some peace?" But her real unease was from Dwain's strong connection to Fox Man, the man found in the Lindow bog. As if Dwain could predict, or maybe wished for, his own death. So of course Fox Man was expected and welcome at Urma's dining room table.

# THE SWAT TEAM

It's likely that in the future no one will remember for sure what "SWAT" stands for, but everyone will remember what they looked like, the shields, the helmets, the Kevlar vests, batons a-ready, or, as is more usual in Shannon's neighbourhood, guns in hand, safeties off.

Shannon should have known she was in a bad spot earlier. And on some level, she did. Often, when her addict haze would ease a bit, she would phone Urma and complain about the blood on the walls of the house she stayed in, the dirty rigs everywhere, and the people she didn't even know walking in and out of her room, using her bed. She'd fuss about her own yellowing eyes. Shannon knew these were not good things. Perhaps more than anyone else invited to Urma's pot luck that night, Shannon understood the importance of good health. Safety, however, was never her strong suit.

So the night she opened her door and found a meeting in progress, an apparent United Nations of drug lords, heavy hitters, and their entourage meeting just outside her bedroom, Shannon chose to stay in and close the door. Her lack of wisdom at that point may have had to do with the fresh fix in her pocket, or an innate territorialism, but she always claimed later it was the need to save her poetry.

When Shannon woke up, she saw the shadow of the helmets and guns through her blind, projected by the yellow streetlight onto her bedroom wall. She rushed to close the window, and immediately phoned Urma. "Urma, the SWAT team is here and I'm going to die and just a sec, let me check." There was silence on the line for a moment. "I'm here alone, so you're my only witness."

"You must be dreaming. It's 3 a.m., Shannon. I have to work in the morning. Hey, where's Eileen?"

"I'm going to make a run for it, Urma, and they will likely shoot me, but I'm leaving all my poetry in the mailbox. Please come and get it for me? Oh please! Oh, gotta go. Good bye. Love you bunches."

"Love you bunches?" Urma was wide awake. She hit Shannon's number. The phone rang.

No one answered.

Eileen stopped by the restaurant on her way to school the next morning.

"Hey, kid! How's your Mom? I got this weird phone call from her last night." Urma automatically drew a glass of milk from the dispenser tap, pulled a cinnamon bun from the display case, and set them both in front of Eileen.

Eileen dropped to one of the counter stools, shrugged and rolled her eyes. "Yeah, we're moving today. The house got raided or something. Mom asked me to bring you these." She slung a garbage bag full of papers onto the counter. "Her writing stuff. She said you'd know what to do with it."

"And what do you think I should do with it?" Urma peeked inside, then wrapped the black plastic tight around the parcel and stuffed it under the counter.

"How should I know? What's so special about saving all those scribbles? Everything else is gone. Our computer, the TV, the DVD player. All seized or something. I haven't even got a change of clothes. And I lost my text book again. My teacher is going to kill me." Eileen's hand swooped across her face, chasing a drop of moisture from the corner of her eye.

"You weren't with you mother last night, right?"

"Right. Or she wouldn't be in the trouble she's in now. But she phoned me and it's all good. She'll be out of jail this morning and we're going to move into a fabulous new suite in the south end and I'll likely be changing schools. I didn't much like this school anyway." She downed the milk, wrapped the pastry in a napkin and loped to the door. "Gotta go. Math this morning."

"Be sure to get me your new address. Or your phone number. Okay?"

Eileen waved through the glass door. Gone.

The restaurant where Urma worked had no sign hanging over the window. It was the place next door to the clinic, the favourite haunt of every user and dealer in town. It wasn't always like that. When Urma first started waitressing, it was a charming retro burger joint, with decent coffee and a mixed clientele. The coffee was still good on the days Urma made it. After her brain injury, her sub-arachnoid haemorrhage, that's what the doctor called it, she was slow and shaky, and had to take orders twice before she could remember them between the table and the kitchen. No one minded. No one cared, really. Although there was always a lot of nervous energy in the place, no one was in any particular hurry. In some ways, Urma's misfortune brought her closer to the community of unfortunates who came for coffee and often stayed longer. Many people shared their stories with her, enjoying Urma's patience, her non-judgemental ear. After the brain injury, Urma was even more like the people who dropped in after the methadone clinic, even more understanding of the weakness of the flesh, the spectre of death.

The first time Urma served her, Shannon had brought Eileen in for a plate of fries. This was five years ago, long before

Urma's injury, and she was now relieved to realize she could remember every detail.

Shannon strolled in and seated herself across from her daughter Eileen as if she'd just been conducted to her table at a five star. She tapped her manicured nails on each item of the dog-eared, laminated menu, reviewing them with her ten-year-old before opting for two colas, fries with gravy.

Shannon's skin was healthy in those days, her straight black hair glossy, her brown eyes clear. Eileen had inherited her mother's elfin grin, her Plains Cree cheekbones, high and round when she smiled, but the girl was blonder than Urma. Shannon wore a designer cut skirt and a feminine but sedate sweater, all in black. Urma guessed this was her parent-teacher interview outfit. Eileen dressed like any middle-class kid in the city. Urma felt dowdy beside them.

"Anything else for you ladies?" Urma asked, setting down the platter of gravy-smothered french fries.

"May we borrow your pen?" Shannon displayed her best ladylike manners.

"My pen?"

"Yes, I see you have a pen behind your ear. May we borrow your pen?"

Urma went through about thirty pens a week. The moment she put one down, someone would palm it, remove the ink refill and use the barrel for snorting something. Or so Urma surmised, as she would often find the dismantled remains down the street or around the corner on her way home. For someone living in the middle of drug central, Urma was pretty clueless about a great deal of what was going on around her. Since the boss bought pens by the bundle, she said "Why not?" and watched as Shannon pulled a handful of napkins out of the tin dispenser and began writing furiously while Eileen savoured each gravy-dipped morsel on their shared plate.

When Urma did her rounds with the coffee pot, she paused to see what Shannon was doing with her pen. Shannon had completed several napkin pages, narrow phrases running down each sheet, emphasized from time to time by a quick sketch: a smiling face, a house, trees. "So, are you an artist?" Urma asked as the pen continued to fly on the delicate paper.

"Sort of." Shannon's dimpled smile. "A poet."

Urma glanced quickly around the almost empty restaurant, nodded her head in an unspoken question, then slid into the booth beside Eileen and began to read the words.

An artist. Like Urma's mother. Urma's mother was delicate, too delicate to handle life's little stresses. Urma had been her mother's sounding board ever since Urma could remember. Mother would burst into Urma's bedroom, weeping, and Urma would listen. She had no choice then, a child of six.

Her mother was a talented artist, but talent is easy. Dedication makes an artist, Urma had learned. Urma's mother was great with inspiration, but not so good with completion and cleanup. Baby Urma learned to walk through passageways of unfinished canvases, open paint tubes. Jars of brushes soaked on the kitchen table beside her cereal bowl. Stacks of potential sculptures formed the walls of the path to the door.

When Mother did finish a work, she became even more frustrated. Her painting and sculptures were not well received. She was never recognized for her talent. Urma commiserated, reassured.

Nor was Mother a hugger. Urma could not remember ever being hugged. Their touch was utilitarian – doing up zippers, knotting scarves, and sometimes Mother would braid Urma's hair into tight, thick ropes.

Urma's mother fell apart after Father's surgery – his heart surgery was a success but his brain was damaged as a result. At first, Mother tried to visit Father in the home, but the visits tapered to weekly, then monthly, and, when Father no longer recognized her at all, she stopped seeing him, except at Christmas and his birthday.

"Hello Dad, how you doing?" Urma asked on her monthly visit.

"Oh, hi. It's so good to see you." He had no clue who she was.

It's a good day. Father had been sitting up, looking through a book – photographs of barns – and now he was shuffling down the antiseptic hallways, looking for a doorway out of the building. Urma guided him to the caged-in patio, to walk the perimeter of the fence. "They forgot to put a gate in this one," he said.

Early in his stay his farmer hands were strong enough to fix that problem by unwrapping the metal strands of the chain link, creating an opening big enough to let himself out onto the prairie. That was a long time ago, and now he simply looked at his hands. Sometimes he couldn't remember how to unwrap a mint candy.

On bad days, he was still in bed at noon, his eyes glazed from the drugs administered that morning. He would not sit up, and shrank away from an unexpected touch. This was the way they needed him to be, manageable. Sometimes he forgot to eat, but they gave him liquid food. He looked like everyone else in the home, many of them already in wheelchairs, vacant eyed and drooling.

Mother couldn't handle the change in him, the strangeness in the way he tried to cling to her – she called it clawing – and his weakness, his fear, when he was supposed to be the strong one. Antidepressants seemed to help her anxiety, but ended her life as an artist. She methodically destroyed all her unfinished work, gave away all that could be salvaged of the materials, and trashed the rest.

She filled her days reading mystery novels and watching detective programs when she wasn't meeting with her lady-friends to play cards.

Now her life was so far away from Urma's that she didn't notice when Urma failed to make her weekly phone calls. Urma could not tell her about the brain haemorrhage. It would have been too much. Mother would have had to increase her dosage of anti-depressants, sleep even more, find even more escapes, and it would have been all Urma's fault. Urma would have felt guilty for giving her mother unbearable stress, of providing her with yet another brain-damaged loved one to worry about, or to avoid worrying about.

She learned through life with her mother how to love art, how to listen without judgement, and how to be a good host.

Was it any wonder Urma immediately felt a bond with Shannon, the poet? Urma had worked the tables of the restaurant next door to the methadone clinic long enough to understand Shannon's weaknesses, but the writing Shannon shared over cola and fries showed Urma a whole person, a unique voice, an authentic heart, and a sharp eye.

*The lady in the restaurant gracious and kind*
*serves french fries on china, cola in crystal*
*makes this ho feel like a queen*
*and her little girl a princess*
*She smiles real, trusts me with a pen*
*reads this poem as if it's a gift*
*The lady in the restaurant gracious and kind*
*has sad and beautiful blue eyes*
*Who is this woman generous and wise*
*Who can she be when she feels*
*everyone's more important than her?*

"Is this about me?" Urma asked Shannon.

Shannon smiled. "Could be."

"You've got the details all wrong," Urma said, seriously.

Shannon watched her with anticipation. Eileen sat up with squared shoulders, ready to defend her mother.

Urma tapped the empty platter on their table. "This is not bone china, you know."

They laughed together for the first time, laughter being the carrier of pleasant surprise, of recognition. "Will you be my new sister?" Shannon asked.

"As it happens I don't have a sister, so that position is currently open. How about a probationary period?" Urma suggested.

"Mom, aren't you already on probation?" Eileen asked Shannon.

"Not that kind of probation, Sweetcakes." Part of Shannon's life would always be hidden from Urma.

Shannon held out her hand. "I'm Shannon, by the way, and this is my lovely daughter, Eileen."

"My name is Urma. Urma with a 'u'. The drinks and fries are on me this time. And, why not?" No one had ever made a work of art about her before. "Sister."

## THE FOX MAN ARRIVES

Urma glimpses her first guest through a smudge in the glass of a wine goblet she holds up to polish.

He wears loose-fitting cotton pantaloons. They appear sometimes white, sometimes with rainbow sheen. An open woven vest reveals a long-necked bird motif that marches across his chest. Around his thick left upper arm, he wears a sleek band of red fox fur. He looks like a sultan out of the Arabian Nights.

"Good evening. I am Fox, here for the Put Luck."

"Pot luck. Pot. It means bring whatever food you like and take your chances at what comes together. But you knew that from the Invitation!" Urma blushes, waving her arms towards the table. "Come in, come on in. You're the first to arrive. Please sit down."

Urma isn't sure how this man came to be standing by her dining room table, but she graciously accepts the heavy loaf of bread wrapped in linen he offers. "Wine or water?"

"Wine, please. It has been some time since I have held a goblet." He is young, surely no more than twenty-five, with surprisingly smooth skin and the kind of square jaw that Urma always considers attractive.

"I have only red. I wasn't sure you would be able to drink."

"Red is fine. I like red." When he smiles she notices with a start that his eye teeth have been sharpened and bear delicate carved designs, birds in flight. "I believe you requested this, as well." He holds out a small vellum scroll, decorated with elegant lettering in browning ink:

*Recipe for Leavened Bread: Have your woman grind grains (avoiding those which have over-wintered in moist conditions, or show any signs of mould) and mix them with yeast, sea salt, honey, water. Form in the shape of the waxing moon and place in the sun until the bread rises. Set on a water-soaked paddle and in the fire until brown.*

Your woman, Urma reads, and smiles at her guest. Apparently a woman's responsibility for domestic labour is hard-wired into this guy.

Urma's table is round, but if there could be a head to such a table, it would be the one facing the broad windows to the west and the sunset. He chooses that place, and eases into the wooden chair as if it were a throne.

With much appreciation, Fox watches Urma pour wine. She pours herself a glass too and sits across from him.

Urma guesses she is entertaining a guest of some antiquity. "Thank you for your presence. Welcome to my home," she says. "I need to know your story." Urma meets Fox's eyes for a heartbeat. "I'm sorry. I know that sounds forward. But I wonder if you can help me? I am missing so many people from my life. I spend my nights being afraid to die and my days being afraid to live. I want to stop being afraid. I want to stop losing people."

"That happens as we age. In my lifetime, I lost almost everyone before I was cast into the bogs."

"You're the bog man! Of course, the fox band! Lindow Man. I've heard about you! I've seen your body in the British Museum." That's one of the reasons she's invited him, of course. And because of Dwain. But with his clothes on, he looks more like an iron-age chieftain.

"It is just a body. Its purpose, to hold my spirit, was completed long ago. It's a little tasteless, isn't it? The display. One would hope for something less institutional, more in keeping with one's station in life." He strokes the fox fur on his arm. His hands are smooth, and his nails trim and clean. "Something more ceremonial perhaps. You no longer have the equivalent in this world. I was born the elder-leader, responsible for all physical and spiritual needs. Our society was built on harvesting the grains in this bread you will eat tonight. Most of the grains no longer exist. When the weather began to change, we became hungry, and many people died. As the leader, I had to as well."

"How did you die?" It is the first time Urma has asked that question in exactly that way, and the words come out a bit faintly even to her ear. "I'm sorry. I mean, was it an accident?"

"Don't be embarrassed. You will want each of us to speak of our deaths, won't you? That's why you've asked us here. Why I have travelled to this faraway place. To appease your curiosity."

"I don't think curiosity would be strong enough. I don't want to die myself quite yet, although I know I will." Urma pauses for a sip of wine.

Fox Man smiles, knowingly. "Before I tell you how I died, may I share with you how I lived?"

"That would be great! Please!"

"May I have some more wine?"

Urma pours wine into his glass. She hasn't anticipated such thirst, but is glad she's bought extra, just in case.

"In those years in the part of the world now called Manchester, the land was very warm, and life was easy. The grain matured every fall and sometimes spring too. There were banks of clay nearby, and we became excellent potters." He pauses to taste the wine. "The beech and oak forests had not yet been cut down for ships and for industry. Most of us lived in simple wooden houses. We had not yet perfected the art of controlling cooking fires in enclosures, as you do now, and so gradually the wooden houses were replaced by earth and stone. My house was built in two layers. I lived upstairs. I had three people living downstairs: my mother, my wife and my daughter. They cared for the grain, the hay and the animals there."

"Cats? Dogs?"

The chieftain shakes his head. "Sheep, pigs, and cattle, and only in the cool season to keep us warm. They were rubbed with sweet grasses every day so they were clean, and we had a drainage canal throughout the settlement for all wastes, including human."

Urma tips the wine bottle over his glass to top it up. "How many people lived under your rule?"

Fox sips from his goblet. His eye teeth glint. "The people were just beginning to settle down into communities. Our home was chosen because it was close to running water, where the limestone and clay met on the hillside. The enclosure included the hill top, for defence, and we dug terraces into the hillside for planting the grains, and for protection. We were a small group by your standards, five hundred. There were other groups — bands or clans — in the area, but not many were as fortunate as we were. We suffered from their envy."

"They attacked you?"

"We were burnt out five times. Five lean years. And then the first snows fell, and the spring waters did not thaw even when the sun was high in the sky. Many of our grains did not survive the cold, or worse, got damp and spoiled. My mother and my wife did their best, but some of our grain went bad. You have heard of ergot?"

Urma nods. What farm girl has not?

"Perhaps you have not experienced the results of ergot poisoning. I lost my family to the inflammation, the excruciating pain in the limbs, the loss of circulation, the rot. First my mother, then my wife. My daughter was only ten years old when I died."

"I'm so sorry." Urma feels her eyes brimming. She was born near water, Shannon had once said, because her eyes so often flooded. "It sounds horrible. Especially not to be there for a child. But I thought you died in ceremony. That's what the Museum thinks."

"They are right. As the weather changed, and disease hit, we started to lose our community. We began fighting among ourselves, and as people became hungrier, and more frightened of the sicknesses, the suffering included bad feelings in the community and about me. As the elder-leader I had no choice but to die many tiny deaths. This is very good wine."

Urma pours into his glass and hers. "Tiny deaths?"

"I underwent all the ways to die. Forced to eat mouldy grain. Beaten. Strangled. Speared. All done very slowly, very formally, before all my people, with them rejoicing. Exposure to the elements. And drowning, of course, in the crushing peat – the final death. No burial. Just the bog. It was believed the more I suffered, the less my people would have to." He smiles.

"It worked for awhile. At least they had hope and courage. But it did not stop the changes. My people became nomads again."

"I'm sorry." Urma sips her wine, and feels the heat creep up her cheeks. I'd better hold off on this a bit, at least until I've eaten, she thinks.

"You have witnessed the leer of death, have you not? And walked away." Fox grins. "We all do it."

Urma chooses not to hear this, moving on to safer ground. "Until recently most people here were travellers. I guess, even my family had to leave Europe and find a better place, after hundreds of years of farming in one spot." Urma had been back to visit Finland, her father's country, thinking at the time it would be like going home. "In Canada most of us are just learning to live here. Even the people who were here first have gone through brutal changes in my lifetime. But we've never had a leader who was willing to die for us."

"Urma, is there anything you're willing to die for?" Fox's eyes crinkle kindly over the rim his glass.

"I've only got one reason to stay here, Fox." Urma pauses for a mouthful of wine. "And once I find her, I'll be ready to die."

As she speaks, she notices a bull-chested man in grey work pants and a clean white shirt approaching the table.

"*Hyva Paiva!*" He chooses a chair facing the south window, and accepts a glass. "Water only for me, *tytta*. Only water."

"Good day to you, too. I know you by your photograph, Mr. Sukanen, and I am very pleased to have you at my table."

"Please, I am Tom. Only the fools in the hospital called me 'Mr.' and they did not say it respectfully. Here, I am pleased to bring you this." He passes her a pottery bowl, steaming with cooked wheat and berries. "*Puolukka Kiisseli,*" he announces. "Made the right way." He passes her a yellowed sheet of newsprint, covered in neat, bold printing, in the smudgy blue of a carpenter's pencil.

> *Lingonberry Soup*
> *Stir in puolukka or cranberries if you must with cold water and sugar. Boil the berries. Thicken with cornstarch, and spoon over wheat cooked in milk.*

"That's the *kiisseli.* It's a dessert. You eat it last." Tom taps the end of the table. "But first you have a sip of the *puolukka* with vodka." He holds up two earthenware jugs. "Do you have real glasses for that?"

"Of course. Tom, this is —"

"Fox," Fox says, looking at Urma, not Tom.

Urma disappears to her kitchen, searching for the proper glassware. All my life running to serve, she thinks. When she returns with three flat-bottomed glasses, Tom is already explaining his world to Fox. "Now, pour us a drink here, girl. I am sorry; she has forgotten all her manners. In this new country they teach them nothing. The women think they have something more here, but they have less. Much less."

At a loss to know what she has done wrong, if anything, Urma smiles politely and pours. "More than that! Don't be stingy, there's lots there. You will like this, Fox. This is best for Finnish pot luck supper."

"And for breakfast and for dinner, too," Urma adds. The Finns seemed to never tire of the bitter fruit.

Puolukka berries were in season when Urma visited her cousin in the old country. The table was flanked with benches. Hand-loomed weavings covered the table in brilliant stripes. Forest-and-lake tapestries brightened and warmed the walls. A massive fireplace-oven divided the kitchen and eating area from the tiny sitting room. The porch was as large as the inside of the house. Benches lined the walls, and from the porch, Urma remembered the door to the wood-burning sauna. The wooden floors were scrubbed perfectly clean. There were two bedrooms, just large enough for a bed and simple shelving. The toilet was an outhouse, by the barns.

*Little cousin* they had called her, and she helped Vaino cut and load turnips, and Johanna make *piparkakku*, spice cookies, and spoon *piima*, stringy yoghurt, into bowls of tiny woodland berries. It was November and already the roads were so slick with ice they could only travel during the middle of the day. That was when the neighbour arrived with his van, bringing bread in exchange for vegetables. Later, they drove Vaino's van to the seashore, exchanging more vegetables for dried fish from the wizened man seated by the wood smoker on the beach. Vaino picked out a special treat. "Eels," he said in his best English. "You like eels." He pulled one out of the brown paper wrapping by the eyes and crunched on the dried fish, as if it were a potato chip.

The countryside was all rocks and poplar, gently rolling, relieved occasionally by small open fields and the oxblood red and sandstone yellow of the Finnish buildings. Even the church in the village was painted yellow.

Fish and berries, salty and fresh. Like the Finns: formal and playful, complex and straightforward, determined and easy-going, silent and boisterous. I didn't understand the contradictions at the time, Urma thinks. She realizes her guests are watching her, bemused, as if they could read her thoughts. Some host, she thinks.

"I'm so glad you two have met here," Urma says. She'd been introduced to both Fox and Tom in museums. Someone had loved them enough, or been curious about their lives enough to enshrine them. Unlike Shannon, or Dwain, or so many of her people, fading from memory, becoming names on stones, and sometimes not even that. "Tom, you have quite a bit in common with Fox."

"Such as? He is not a working man. And possibly not a socialist. Nor an inventor. I am all these things." Tom spreads out his thick, heavily scarred fingers for her to see.

"Tom built a ship with his own two hands," Urma says to Fox. "An ocean-going ship cold-forged out of metal in Big Valley, seventeen miles from the Saskatchewan River and thousands of miles from the ocean. My father remembers hearing the pounding from our farm, five miles away." The Finns formed communities when they came to Canada, and relied on each other to navigate the often bewildering world of the English. Not too near each other, though. A nationality thriving on differences.

"And no royalty," Tom continues from Urma's thoughts.

"Each man is responsible for his own fortune, his own failure."

"And each woman," Urma adds, eagerly.

"And each woman," Tom says each word slowly. Urma can't tell whether he is being polite or emphatic. Tom points at Fox. "We didn't need any figurehead, any pampered royalty."

"Excuse me," Fox leans toward Tom, placing his wine glass on the table very carefully. "I died for my people, for their future."

"And I died for my dream." Tom glares at Fox an uncomfortable moment, then turns to Urma. "It was hard work, and all I had to eat for the last few winters was cooked wheat like that." He points to the dish and then to Urma. "Without the berries."

An obsession, Urma thinks. The berries and the dream. She remembers the stories of Tom's last years, how the Finnish immigrant's crops had failed, as everyone's did in the 1930's, how he had abandoned his shack in the Coteau hills to live in the hull of the iron ship, how he had tried to drag it to the Saskatchewan river, piece by piece, his horses collapsing under the strain, how he had suffered in the winters, and finally lost his health. The neighbours say he stopped talking, stopped responding. He was finally taken to North Battleford Mental Hospital, where he died.

"Bad grain, I suspect," Fox says, knowingly.

"I was never crazy." Tom thumps the table with his thick fist. "Why they put me in a place like that? I just want to finish my work, take my ship, go home. That's not crazy. And they didn't even speak my language."

Urma blinks, recalling her own months of relative silence after her injury. Maybe she is crazy. At least Tom had a dream. "But it was just after the great drought, and lots of old bachelors ended up in the Hospital." She couldn't say asylum.

"I was not a bachelor. My family was waiting for me, maybe. And I was not old."

Fox is thoroughly enjoying the conversation. "You would have been younger than Urma, perhaps, when you died?"

"Exactly."

"And then your body was exhumed and moved into a museum." Urma shudders, recalling her visit to the country museum near Moose Jaw built in honour of Tom Sukanen. What remained of the ship and Tom's other inventions were on display. His new grave lay just off the starboard bow of his ship.

"At least your body's not in the open, in a glass case."

"It's just a body," Tom says, and Fox nods.

"And you never made it home," Urma adds.

"Yes I did."

"So you see, all that outrage you've been feeling on our behalf, on behalf of our bodies, can be released now." Fox smiles, and then smiles even more broadly at someone behind Urma. She turns to greet Shannon and Dwain.

"Oh my god, Shannon!" Urma leaps from her chair, but stops herself just before hugging her old friend. "You look great. Is it okay to touch you?"

"I think so. I haven't touched a living person yet."

"I did. Or tried." Dwain says. Dwain had died before Shannon, in the early days of their love. He must have missed Shannon almost as much as she missed him, Urma decides.

"And you get a hug too." Urma slides their casserole dishes to the centre of the table, and throws her arms around both of them.

"I guess it only works if they know you're here," Dwain says to Shannon. "Now we know."

"Shannon, this is wonderful!" Urma waves at her old friend's flowing hair and catches a fringe of the turquoise gown between her fingers.

"Finally I get to choose whatever I want to wear and no one calls me on it. And I've found my love, as you see. Have you, Urma?"

"If I had, would I be hanging around with dead people?" Urma grins. "Okay, maybe I would, anyway. Thanks for the food, folks. Lasagna, Dwain? I didn't know you were Italian."

"Italian? Oh, no, I just like the layers. But it's got to be well set. I hate it when the edges slip all over. You'll have to try this one. And Shannon's crab apples." Dwain presents Urma with a sheaf of napkins, ball point ink scrawled in columns on each narrow fold, interspersed with quick, comical sketches.

### Grandma's Spinach, Beef and Cheese Lasagna

*Layer lightly cooked lasagna noodles with ground beef browned in tomatoes, oregano and basil, drained steamed spinach and drained cottage cheese in a roaster. End with noodles and smother with grated mozzarella and Parmesan. Bake until hot and set 30–45 minutes in a standard oven.*

### Crab Apple Crumble

*Core and clean blossom from apples. Quarter into casserole dish, squeeze ½ lemon and sprinkle with lemon zest, cinnamon and nutmeg. Stir in brown sugar to taste — no more than ½ cup. Melt ½ cup butter; mix with ¾ cup of sugar and 1½ cups of rolled oats (more if they are 'quick oats'). Spread and pat on top of apples. Pop in the oven with the Lasagna, and leave in until the fruit is cooked. Serve hot or cold.*

"I think we'll serve this hot. Crab apples, Shannon? I guess this is a healthy transition." Urma waves at the table. "Shannon, Dwain, this is Tom, and I think you know Fox."

Tom stands to shake hands with each of them. Dwain holds out his hand to Fox and then, as Fox stands, moves in for a bear hug. "That's my man!" Dwain says. "Shannon, this is Fox Man, my old friend!"

Fox beams, his odd teeth a bit eerie in the dusk light. "I'm so pleased you remember me."

"Remember you? We're brothers in the earth, Fox."

Three months before he died, Dwain met Shannon.

Before Shannon, Dwain's experience with drugs amounted to beers on the weekend, and an aspirin for pain. He had never even seen anyone smoke marijuana, except on TV. Shannon was attempting a traditional jig on the dance floor of his usual bar, and laughing at her own silly efforts. When she noticed him noticing her, everything went slow motion, as if he were looking through a camera, and maybe his heart slowed down for a moment too. She wasted no time coming over and sitting down. Bold, he'd thought then.

"Buy me a drink," she said, resting her hand on his shoulder and leaning toward his face so he could smell her hair, sweet and fresh as a hay meadow.

"No problem, miss." Dwain waved down the waitress, who frowned at Shannon, but took Dwain's order for a rum and coke, with a twist of lime.

She pulled him to the dance floor and they moved together, once he got the stiff-leggedness, the self-conscious shuffle out of the way. The jukebox played all the old favourites, *Orange Blossom Special, King of the Road, Your Cheating Heart.*

They two-stepped, polka'd and waltzed skin to skin. If there were danger signs, he disregarded them.

In the enthusiasm of the moment, Dwain had no warning of how much energy and space a person like Shannon could take. In Dwain's way of thinking, a girl and a guy should be loyal and true. What happens in the past is one thing, but once you're together, you owe it to each other at least to be honest.

If Shannon were able to, she would have told him how difficult – perhaps inconceivable – it is to be honest and an addict. The two concepts just don't work together. To survive as an addict, you deceive: first oneself, and then everyone else. "Just one more." "Never again." "A little won't hurt." And even "One day at a time." Shannon had said them all, and the last was the biggest lie. Not one day, or even one hour, but one trillionth of a second at a time. The very basis of the molecule, the tiniest quark of who she was as a person, would have to change fundamentally in order to put someone else's needs first. Shannon would have to re-learn pleasure – what it means and why she needs it. To acknowledge temptation and accept a life of resisting temptation is to live a life of denial, when her problem began with an exceptional need in the first place.

No one, not even a lover, not even a loved one, can fill that need.

Dwain woke up in the wee hours of Monday morning, after that first weekend together, to see Shannon bent over a needle on her thigh. Yes, he'd seen the scars, the collapsed veins, but he just didn't want to know. "Shannon?"

"Dwain, there are a few things about me you should know." She turned to stroke his chest and stomach, but her words slurred and stumbled. "You know, you know, I'm bad. Really, really bad. Bad for you, my love. I do this." She pointed at her arm, at the track marks on her thighs. "I do this, and I'd do anything for this, and I do everything for this. I sell me, my body. And I don't do it for love, like with you. I do it for this."

Dwain sat up, pushed her hand away. "So you have sex with other men for money?"

Shannon nodded emphatically. Her eyes gleamed with tears. "For this."

"God, how could I be so blind?" Dwain was out of bed, pulling on his jeans, to hell with the socks, pulling on his boots and grabbing his shirt.

He walked ten miles that night, through the neighbourhood where Shannon lived, through downtown, and to the prairie edge of the city and back, before he collapsed on the couch of his bachelor apartment. He was treating his blisters when the phone rang the next afternoon. Shannon.

"Dwain, I love you." Crying.

"You lied to me, Shannon. You lied about everything. You're still lying. You don't know how to do anything else."

"I know. I know. I did. But I do love you. It's true."

"So you say. But your drugs will come first."

"No, no I can kick this. I've quit lots of times."

Dwain laughed out loud, a bitter sound. "Look, I need some time to think."

Dwain stayed away for a week, and read everything he could on addiction, from Deepak Chopra to Bill's Big Book. He was just a country boy, but maybe because he'd seen the deterioration of rural life, the way many of his neighbours had chosen the bottle as companion, addiction turned out to be nothing new. Dwain made a decision then. Not based on anything she said, an addict's truth, but on what he felt. He walked over to the house she shared with an ever-changing cast of men and women, most of them younger than either Dwain or Shannon. She was like the house mother there, he had thought at one time. Some house mother. But one of them was her daughter, Eileen. Dwain had only met her in passing, but he was worried about Eileen, and decided he'd try to befriend that little girl as well. He knocked on the door, not knowing whether Shannon would be alone, or in any shape to see him.

Eileen peeked out first before sliding the chains someone had screwed into the wooden door frames. "You're back."

"Hi, Eileen. How was school this week?" What else do you ask a kid? What was she, maybe fourteen?

"Didn't go." She left him standing in the doorway and sat down on the rugged couch, completely focused on the television, where people were screaming and running away from groaning zombies.

"Is your mom in?"

Eileen didn't move her eyes from the screen. "In there." She pointed with her bottom lip towards a closed door.

*Is she alone?* he wanted to ask, but how do you ask a child a question like that? Dwain knocked, and cautiously turned the scarred handle. "Shannon?"

"Who is it?" Gruff, abrupt, angry. It didn't sound like Shannon, or it sounded like a different Shannon, one he didn't want to know.

"It's Dwain, Shannon."

"Oh god. Just a minute!" Her melodic voice had returned, and in a moment, a hair brush still in her hand, she opened the door to him, sliding herself into his arms. "I missed you! It's been six and a half days! Are you done thinking?"

Dwain pushed her away from him, his hands on her shoulders, and stared intently into her eyes.

"Look, I'm straight." She smiled the dimpled smile that had made a hard path a bit easier. "I'm writing poetry. Come see. Love poetry." The bed and floor were covered with sheets of paper, each crammed with columns of words, marred with cross-outs and marginal corrections. Her signature drawings scrawled in the spaces near the title, and beside the bottom of each page, where she'd printed her name and the date.

"Wow, you've been busy." They stepped into the room, and his hands were on her back, pulling her into a kiss before he could stop himself. "Whoa. We've got to talk. Sit down, okay?" he said.

Shannon cleared the papers from the bed and flounced down, patting the space beside her.

Dwain had to get this out in one go. Before he got distracted. But it wasn't the kind of thing he could have said in a phone call. "Shannon, you will die of this. Maybe from the drugs, maybe from the men. That makes me sad." Dwain cleared his throat. He could just be another john to her, another customer. He could just use her and walk out of here and not come back. Dwain knew that would be much easier.

Shannon was holding her breath.

"Look, you're an addict. I don't know if you can change, if you want to change." Don't you ever start a relationship expecting the other person to change, his dad always said, because they won't. Another thing his dad had said, though, was live for the moment.

Shannon was staring at her red-painted toes. He touched her cheek and she turned to him. "I haven't got time to be unhappy, so let's have some fun. And I'll love you, Shannon. You will feel loved."

She made one of those high pitched sounds of delight usually heard from the mouths of children and returned his hug. "I'll be so good to you. You'll see."

"First let's see some of this poetry of yours."

"Later," Shannon said, pushing the door firmly shut and lifting her sweater over her head.

To his and Shannon's utter delight, they found the pleasure theory worked sometimes. When Shannon felt the need for drugs, which could be when she was hungry, or tired, or scared, or excited, she and Dwain would find other ways of providing the hit she needed. Some of it involved learning when she needed a hug, when she needed massage or when sex was the best focus. Sometimes she went a week drug-free, well, except for the methadone. Of course, then Shannon would feel like celebrating, which took them back to where they started. At one point, Shannon had a poem published in a literary magazine. Urma celebrated with her by going to a movie, but after the buoyancy of success came the doubt, the fear of worthiness. Her recovery was like peeling a vegetable and watching the new colour leach away before applying the knife to another layer. Dwain couldn't be there all the time. All too soon he wasn't there for her at all. Soon enough, he had to return to the crumbling edge of the trench.

Dwain's last job was digging a water drainage system for a farm corporation. It was a pig operation, and the stench of the manure mixed with rotting carcasses would not scrub off in the shower. People work in those places. Animals live there, if you could call it a life. He had to ask why there were so many dead animals, but the owner just shrugged.

"You expect some loss in an operation this size."

The owner was a businessman who had never worked in a farm yard, but knew how to manage money and human resources. "The humane treatment of product does not enter into the equation," he said.

Neither did the safe disposal of wastes, Dwain thought.

"The inspectors want us to have our own system, now. They're worried about their precious river," he told Dwain. "So we want you to make it so."

Dwain wasn't an engineer, but he could see that any system he dug in the week he was there was for show only. The trench he was asked to dig on Friday would take everything back to the river anyway, but below the surface. It wasn't a good arrangement – it would almost certainly be blocked within a year, and if it sprang a leak, it would poison the water source for the entire region. But, as the manager explained, "No one lives out here anymore anyway, except my livestock, a few deer, coyotes, and some retired farmers who get their water from town. Pigs and cattle can drink anything."

At four-thirty Friday afternoon, Dwain stood at the edge of the trench, looking ten feet down, where the pipe was already being covered by loose soil from the sides and sliding mud. Rain pelted the peak of his ball cap. He was soaked and tired and wanted to go home. But he could see it; they all could. There was a kink in the plastic pipe. They had to fix it before they could back-fill the trench. Someone had to go down there.

"Don't look at me," the backhaul operator said. "I've seen this before. It's not safe."

"Alright, we'll leave it until Monday. Maybe it'll be drier by then." Dwain hated to have to take the trip out again. The expense would eat into his earnings.

"Still won't be safe. Too narrow. Why didn't he have us bank this up properly in the first place?"

"Because it's not supposed to be there in the first place." Dwain took his cap off and slapped it on his pant legs. Water streamed down his forehead, plastering his thinning hair to his skull. He swung around and walked with his long-legged farmer stride to the farm office to talk to the man.

"What a bunch of inept yokels! You let a little rain stop you? Well, if you think I'm going to pay you one more day's work for this job, you're nuts." The manager snapped a fistful of envelopes on his desk top. "And if you leave that trench open, you're liable if anyone or anything falls into it." His attention returned to the paperwork on his desk and Dwain was dismissed.

"Well, that went better than I expected," Dwain said to the backhaul operator as he climbed into the half ton and headed into the city.

When he arrived, freshly showered, at Shannon's place he found Shannon asleep on her bed. He couldn't wake her up, even when he shook her. Breathing, but cold. He climbed into bed and held her until they were both warm. That was their third to last night together.

# METHADONE BLUES – PLAYING WITH THE FORMULA

Shannon loved to be high. That was just the truth. Although Dwain tried to help, and Eileen was silently hopeful, and Urma, her sister/friend, was cheering for her, in her addict's heart Shannon knew she would drop anyone and everyone in a flash for a stash.

There was more than one methadone clinic in the city, but Shannon's was in her neighbourhood, next door to the restaurant where Urma waitressed, right by a pharmacy, one block from the nightclubs. It was the hangout for street workers like herself, gang members, ex-cons, and lots of kids. In fact, Shannon was one of the older people in every week to pick up her medication.

Dwain drove her to the clinic, then waited outside. The front of the clinic was all glass so you could always see who was coming or going, who was waiting inside. All addicts, of course. Two mothers with children in strollers waited their turn. A couple of bold-faced teenaged girls sat on the reception desk, showing off their legs to the flustered man behind the counter.

A wiry guy with a pocked complexion walked in, spun around and out quickly and went into the restaurant next door, just letting people know he was open for business. Everyone noticed him, and everyone would go next door as soon as they finished their business here. Everyone but Shannon, because Dwain was waiting for her. She couldn't help but feel a burn of impatience. Why couldn't he just leave her alone for a minute. Didn't he trust her? She sat on one of the plastic waiting room chairs, and stared at the anti-drug posters covering every surface of the walls. She could have posed for one of them. That would have been a laugh. Were those people paid for that work? Were they really users?

When her number came up, Shannon walked with as much dignity as possible to the reception. The girls very reluctantly moved their legs, but remained seated, so she could barely see the red-faced man behind the desk, let alone effectively argue with him when he told her "I'm sorry, Shannon. We can't give you this week's treatment unless you give us a urine sample." He handed her a small jar and pointed to the washroom.

"Oh, no! Really, I wish I'd known about this sooner!" She lowered her voice and her lashes "I just went to the washroom. I couldn't possibly piss now. I'll have to go and drink some coffee or something next door. You wouldn't have a couple dollars for that, would you?"

No, he didn't, and the girls on the desk giggled. Shannon handed one of them the jar. "Here, you use this," and walked out. Where could she find someone to help? Clearly she couldn't give. It would show she'd been messing with the formula, and mixing her drugs, and they'd cut her off. She'd used her period as an excuse last time, but if they were writing things down, they'd know this wasn't her moon again. She needed someone who would have a clear sample, with only methadone showing. She stuck her head in the restaurant. The skinny little pusher was already dealing with a line up. No one clean in there except Urma. No way she would help Shannon get her poison. If she were sure they couldn't tell the difference between male and female samples, she'd slip Dwain a bit of methadone and ask him to help. But he was way too straight.

She slammed the car door, clearly upset. "They won't give me any, they've cut me off!" she said to Dwain.

"Just like that? What about withdrawal? What about the supposedly fatal results of stopping suddenly? What about the program they gave you? You go right back in there and insist on your rights!"

Shannon hung her head.

"Right, they asked for another test, and you refused. I get it."

"Let's check back later. It might be a different guy at the desk." And there always was someone who would give her 'just one more chance'. Shannon always saved a bit extra anyway, in case she got ripped off or refused, or just needed a bit more that day.

She had followed their program exactly one week. Methadone had put her to sleep while riding the city bus. She was so embarrassed, having gone full circle, that she swore she'd never take a bus again. It put her to sleep when she was waiting for her daughter's parent-teacher interview. Eileen was furious with her for a week after. Methadone put her to sleep in the bar, which was not safe, which was a place where she needed all her skill and watchfulness in order to avoid enemies and do business. After falling asleep in all the wrong places, she decided it was safer to just take a little bit less and so she diluted, mixed and matched the level of concentration to her mood. Too much and she'd be a zombie. Too little and she'd be in pain. There were particular levels of methadone appropriate for partying with the family, for powwows, and for participation in the sun dance.

# Eileen at the Pow Wow

Despite all her brains at school, Eileen knew almost nothing about being a traditional Indian woman. She just hadn't had much time with her kokum and the family still living on the reservation. In fact, differences of opinion about how Eileen was being raised had made her and Shannon's few visits to their home reserve, now a Nation, stressful. Shannon did recognize that she needed some help with Eileen, though. The girl was becoming a young woman. Shannon's opportunities to reach and teach the child were becoming limited, but maybe Eileen would listen to Kokum. Shannon's mother was a spiritual lady.

No one can deny the power of the drums. At powwows, Shannon was always one of the first in her family to grab her shawl and circle the dance ground in the stately traditional women's dance. She never hesitated, either, to encourage the more energetic dancers, particularly the chicken dancers, with their long lean legs and proud head movements. Her home reserve had modest powwows, but the pageantry was glorious. Men's chests gleamed with intricate bone and quill work, their moccasins beaded in the traditional geometry of the plains, and often small bells swung from their ankles. Some of the dancers carried turtle shell rattles or wing feathers. The costumes combined every shade of the rainbow, from iridescent purple and turquoise to fuchsia and scarlet to forest green and lemon yellow; the brighter the better. The head dresses and bustles were works of art, adorned with hawk, owl and eagle feathers, wolf, coyote and badger skins, and porcupine quills. The women's shawls, fringed, appliquéd and embroidered, swung in gracious drapes from their arms. Their modest skirts skimmed the tops of their moccasins. The jingle dancers' tin bells covered the bottom third of their skirts, crashing together to the rhythm of the dance. Hoots of encouragement mingled with the wail of the singers as they drummed the real heartbeat of the nation. Only a very hard person would be unmoved by the physical thrill, by the music. Or a teenager with an mp3 player and permanent ear buds. Eileen rocked to her own music and no one else's.

"Come dance with me, my girl," Shannon begged Eileen, who stood stony faced at the edge of the powwow grounds. The girl pulled the hood of her sweater over her face and flipped an unlit cigarette between her fingers.

"Please. Show your kokum you still know how to do this." Shannon gestured at the elderly woman seated in a lawn chair a few yards down, a blanket over her knees. "It will make her so proud. And me."

"No. I'm going for a walk." Eileen swung away from her mother, and the dancers, veering towards the trailers where they sold hamburgers, bead work, and scratch tickets.

Shannon straightened her back and entered the dance ground, stepping in stately rhythm as she made her way over to where Kokum watched with eagle eyes.

Kokum held a fringed shawl over her folded arms. "Where is my granddaughter?" She stood, taking the elbow of a slightly younger woman who paused before her, respectfully.

"Gone for a walk." Shannon shrugged.

"Bring her to me." Kokum turned and stepped with dignity and grace into the wheel of dancers.

Shannon scanned the verge of the grounds, fingering the silken tassels of her own shawl, a turquoise bird opening its lovely wings. Eileen had found two other teenagers. The three were huddled in a shady corner, sharing a cigarette. Shannon bit her lip and walked towards her daughter in the most indirect way possible, stopping to exchange greetings with three or four cousins and an old friend along the way. Finally, as if by accident, she stood beside Eileen. *When did her girl get so big?* Shannon thought. Eileen was at least an inch taller than her mother and likely fifteen pounds heavier. Solid and somehow throwing a dark energy that made Shannon feel tired.

"Oh, hello, my girl! Hello." Shannon shook hands with each of Eileen's friends. "Eileen, your kokum wants you."

"Doesn't look like it to me." Eileen shrank from Shannon's touch on her arm.

"She has asked me to bring you to her." No one refused a request from Kokum. Eileen reluctantly followed her mother, refusing to link arms with her or enter the dance.

Kokum paused at the edge of the dance grounds and waited for her granddaughter. "Shannon, give this girl a shawl. She's going to dance with me."

Shannon passed the turquoise shawl to Eileen, adjusting it carefully. "Don't drag it in the dust!"

Eileen was doing her best to shrink, to disappear. "I don't know how to dance, Grandma! Dance with Mom. She likes it."

"And you don't? Here, take my arm." And they were off, leaving Shannon standing uncertainly.

"You, my girl, are from a family of dancers," Kokum said. "You don't have to know how to dance. You just have to remember."

"Okay, but I forget how." Eileen walked stiffly at her kokum's side.

"Take those things out of your ears, and hear the drums. Hold my arm and let your feet go. No one is watching you."

"Everyone is so watching me," Eileen said. "I hate being so blonde. I hate being so big. I hate being here with Mom."

Kokum tightened her lips and looked straight ahead for almost a full song. "They will do one more traditional. If anyone is watching you, they will think you are a fine child for dancing with your grandmother. They will think you are a good dancer. And they will think you are becoming a beautiful young woman."

Eileen was beginning to enjoy the dance, in spite of herself. "I'll go around with you one more time, Kokum."

"That would be good. And just remember, you are the only one judging you. No one worthy of your time will condemn you for what you can't help. Don't condemn yourself. Or your mother."

"I just don't feel like I fit in here. I don't belong."

"This is your mother's home and your grandmother's – my home and the home of all our ancestors. This is the only place where you will always belong. And so does your mother. There is not a family in this reserve without problems. The only way to be strong in the face of our troubles is to stand together. Do not be afraid of the traditional way, Eileen. We will ask your mother to join us."

Shannon had not spent much time alone. She stood on the verge of the earthen dance ground, laughing with a muscular young dancer. He had a shock of black and white feathers sprouting from the top of his head and his bustle, and wore bells on each ankle. His chest was covered with a bone breastplate, beaded in yellow and purple.

"I'll join you guys!" Shannon called eagerly as Kokum and Eileen came by where she stood, and then "Eileen, this is your cousin Roger. He's a fancy dancer."

Roger stepped forward to shake Kokum's hand and then Eileen's. Eileen's face dimpled into a reasonable facsimile of her mother's smile. "I'll see you later, I hope," she said.

"I hope so too." Roger folded finely muscled arms over his chest and beamed a heart-quickening smile Eileen's way.

As the women danced away Eileen whispered, "Mom, is he really my cousin?"

# Urma at the Sun Dance

A year before Shannon died, she invited Urma to the sun dance. Urma was honoured. She knew it was serious business, spiritual and ceremonial, unlike the competitive cabaret of the powwow. The sound of jingles was replaced by eagle whistles; the beaded costumes were replaced by practical, simple, and comfortable cotton. The women were expected to wear long skirts. A few of the men wore ribbon shirts and a few of them were shirtless – showing the scars from previous sun dances. The circus atmosphere was replaced with a circumspect, formal attitude. At sunrise the dancers took their places in their blanket-draped stalls, the poplar branches forming a solid ring of solitary dancing spaces, circling the central pole of the arbour.

The dancers did not eat or drink for the duration of the dance – sometimes two days, sometimes four. They say the second day is always the worst, but that by the evening of that day, you can always count on rain. If it falls from the sky you can drink it. Inside the circle formed by the dancers' stalls around the central tree, the elders sat at the head, facing the opening, the drummers to their left. The members of the community sat in front of the stalls, women to the right of the door, men to the left, backs to the dancers, faces to the pole. The tree became wrapped, as the days went on, with gifts of coloured broadcloth. Embers of burning sweetgrass and sage were brought to the base of the pole every so often. The air smelled pure and clean.

Shannon knew one does not just arrive at the sun dance announcing one's intentions to dance. There are months of purification, singing, and taking advice from elders, and weeks of restricted diet before the dance. A male family member must also be prepared to make the dancer's stall and provide a whistle. When these precautions are not taken, the dancer may bring sickness on him or her self, on loved ones and the community.

Shannon sweet-talked her way into the sun dance without any preparation. "Uncle!" she breathed on the phone, the night she decided to dance. "How are you?"

Her uncle was no fool, but was good-natured enough to be charmed. Besides, like most people, he wanted to believe the best of Shannon. Yes, he would help with the building of the stall. Yes, she could use his eagle whistle for her dance. But Shannon had to convince the elder first.

The elder agreed to meet with Shannon at dusk the night before she hoped to dance, and again at dawn. Urma and Eileen set up their tent while Shannon walked sedately across the ceremonial grounds to where the men stood in a fog of smudge.

"What do you think will happen?" Eileen asked.

"She'll promise the elder she's been good, that she will behave, likely." Urma was pounding tent pegs into the ground.

"I know those guys," Eileen said. "They won't believe her. I bet they'll make some reverse curse on her. You know, to protect everyone else in case she screws up."

"Your mom won't screw up. Besides, we're here to help her, right?"

Whatever happened that night, Shannon returned to the tent glowing with excitement.

The elder greeted Shannon in the morning with a list of all the things she could not do. For Shannon the one thing that rankled was the oath not to write about what she saw.

The elders had agreed to let her dance.

And she did, with dedication.

Urma and Eileen stayed with her, backs up against her stall. Urma knew the sun dance had been documented, and even photographed. The artists likely had approval from elders to proceed, and they were, without exception, male. A woman writer would cause quite a stir. Urma knew Shannon would write a poem about her dancing.

Urma had a lot of time to think about this over the two days Shannon danced. Eileen and Kokum sat beside her from time to time, checking in, but Urma was steadfast in her support and mesmerized by the drumming, by the breath of the eagle whistles. She was fasting, in support of the dancers, too.

When the rain began to fall at dusk on the second day, Urma opened her mouth like the dancers and drank the raindrops. She left for their tent quickly, not able to talk. Her skin smelled sweet, and her heart felt open: the heart blood pulsed in her temples like the drums; her life blood and, two years later, almost her death.

Shannon returned after dark, Eileen in tow. "What an amazing natural high! I'd like to stay like this forever!" Shannon flung herself on the mound of sleeping bags.

Eileen picked up the axe, and left without a word. Urma could hear her chipping and pounding at the firewood just outside the tent.

Shannon nodded at the door. "Eileen's in her moon. She can't go into the arbour now."

Urma shook her head. "But she's your daughter. Don't you need her there by you?"

"And she can't take part in the feast or touch the food. She'll be fine with the other women," Shannon said.

Eileen chopped a lot of wood that night. Shannon fell asleep long before her daughter re-entered their tent. Urma was awake, wincing at each axe blow.

"Hey, Eileen, do you think we have enough firewood now?" Urma teased.

Eileen sat on the edge of her sleeping bag, digging a hole in the floor with a twig. "This is bullshit," she said. "First she makes me stay out here all weekend and then she makes me stay away. She wouldn't even let me bring my music or my games. What am I going to do all day? Listen to the old ladies?"

Urma smiled. "You could do worse, kid." But Eileen kept a sullen distance from the rest of the women outside the arbour.

Urma has relived the details of those four days hundreds of times since. Was Eileen right? Did the elders do a reverse curse? Did they call down their own misfortune? Was the sun dance the cause, or a symptom of the way things were going to unfold?

Urma also had a few questions for Kokum about protocol, which she felt best about asking in the safety of the restaurant, about a week after the sun dance.

"We're not allowed to show our legs in a ceremony, right?" Urma was cleaning the counter at work, and visiting with Shannon, Eileen, and Kokum, having just served them a refill of coffee and cleared the dishes from their lunch of veal cutlets.

Kokum nodded. "Because women are so powerful we are not allowed to open our legs when we sit at the sun dance. We are too powerful to step over a man in ceremony. Too powerful to attend weddings, feasts, funerals, dances or any ceremony during our moon, nor prepare any ceremonial food, nor touch any men involved with ceremony."

Shannon grimaced. "I'm sorry, Kokum, but I wouldn't make a good traditional Cree woman."

"Nor me." Urma laughed.

"Never mind," Kokum said, dabbing her mouth with a paper napkin. "At least it gives you a rest once a month. From men."

Kokum arrives at Urma's dining room table quietly, and stands for a few moments behind Shannon before she speaks.

"It's so good to see you, my girl," Kokum says to Shannon.

Shannon leaps up, gives her an enthusiastic hug.

Kokum turns from Shannon's embrace. "And to see you, Urma," she says. "It is good for you to have invited an elder to such a gathering."

"Welcome! But, Kokum, I think Fox here might be a bit older than you," Urma says.

"Fox, I am Marie Anne Bear, daughter of John Pierre Bear and Lucy Bellgarde MacDonald. I am pleased to meet you."

Fox stands and sweeps down in an elegant bow. "It is my extreme pleasure, Madame."

"You may call me Kokum, Grandmother in my language."

"I am honoured." Fox stands until Kokum sits down, a gesture of respect expected but not often enough bestowed on her during her life on this earth.

So, this is not just Eileen's kokum. An elder, she'd said. Urma's stomach churns; she is always getting the protocol wrong. Even a dead elder – well maybe especially a dead elder – will require some cloth, some tobacco, some sage or sweetgrass in exchange for her presence. Urma has been at enough ceremonies to know this. Kokum sits beside Fox at the head of the table, between Fox and Tom. On her lap is a flat, thick package wrapped in a plastic grocery bag. Urma knows that shape. Her mouth waters.

"This is for you, my girl," Kokum says to Urma, holding a square of white paper.

On a simple recipe card in her plain script, Kokum had written:

### Kokum's Bannock

*Put lots of wheat flour in a big bowl, about six scoops. Add a little bit of baking powder (2 ½ tbsp) and apisis salt (a little salt) and then some sominis (raisins) if you want to. Add enough water and oil to mix it until it is just right (about 4 cups water and ½ cup oil, or more for softer bannock). Stir and add more flour, so it's not too sticky, but soft enough to knead. Don't add any more flour now. Knead just a little, until it's ready. Put it in the pan, poke it with a fork and bake it until it is done (at 450, about 20 minutes). Never oil the pan. If you want fry bread, put it in oil instead, piece by piece.*

Kokum had even spent an afternoon baking with Urma and Eileen, showing them what 'just right' meant, but Urma's attempts were heavy or sodden, never the excellent loaf she sees before her now, which she will not be likely to taste unless she is able to come up with a proper protocol gift. "I'm making some tea, Kokum. I'll be right back."

Urma runs to her bedroom. Think, Urma, think. What would work? It has to be something with meaning. A three-foot length from a bolt of white cotton in the top shelf of her closet will do for the tie-up, but it has been a long time since she's even allowed tobacco into her house. The braid of sweetgrass from Shannon's funeral was still unlit. She had not been able to burn it. It just might do. Folding the braid into the cotton feels exactly right.

Urma enters the dining room with the gift, and smiles as she presents it to Kokum.

"So, I see you haven't forgotten your manners entirely," Kokum says, accepting the broadcloth. "But who has said you may use white cloth, Urma?"

Urma blushes. "Please accept this gift and provide me with the proper guidance," she says.

Kokum laughs. "Well, since white is my colour, I will accept this from you. From now on, though, you should wrap such things in the colour of your family."

"And if my family has no colour?"

"Is that what you need me here for? To learn about your family? You may use green as your colour, then, until you find your family. Now, would you like some bannock?"

Urma is easing the bannock onto a cutting board when Roger appears.

When Roger was alive, he was Shannon's cousin, the fancy dancer, and a close friend of Eileen's. Urma knew him as the painter.

Roger brought his art in a battered cardboard portfolio to the businesses near the methadone clinic, selling his paintings to the doctors, the pharmacist, and, on pay days, to the waitresses at the restaurant. He often stopped to visit Urma, and they'd begun a dialogue about perception – his as a painter and dancer, and Urma's as a person who used to be able to see much better.

That's right, Urma remembers. Her vision was not perfect even before. Part of her vision never cleared after the haemorrhage. A fog. Ironic. She's always loved misty weather, walking in uncertainty through the hills, down the prairie paths, the way she felt safe and protected in the ice fog that clung to the low places sometimes in the winter, the dense blankets like lowered clouds in the early spring, and how sounds arrived clearer and more intimately, almost as if this bird or that scurrying in the leaves were sounds for her alone.

"And what do you see that you don't want to acknowledge?" Roger had asked her.

Roger always saw too much. He never missed a nuance, a facial tic, a wave of a wrist or a gathering of a fist. He observed, processed, obsessed, and in the end, wanted to run away, to find his own fog where no one was beaten, no one was bullied, no one was put down and ignored, where the bouncer didn't challenge him, where the security officer in Canadian Tire didn't question his right to purchase items in every aisle, where the doorman didn't question his right to enter his own art show, where he could function in isolation from everyone who had come before him or after him. But he had, by creating his own blurry world, also fulfilled everyone's expectations. Well, almost. Urma and Eileen, and Shannon, when she was alive, had other hopes for him. Maybe even plans. A better sales system. A show in a gallery. Maybe an agent. When he was alive.

On the walls in Urma's dining room hang two of his paintings. Since he shares Kokum's tradition, Urma knows his name should not be mentioned, photographs of his face should be turned to the wall, and that it will not be seen as kind, but rather as an interruption to his journey to the four directions, if he is called away like this from his final learnings with the ancestors before a year has passed from the date of his death. Urma has business with him, though.

Kokum is the first to see him. "You cannot be here," she says. "You have no time. Go now, you're no longer part of this lady's world."

"Kokum, it's okay. I invited him," Urma says.

"And you know better, Urma." Kokum crosses her arms over her breasts, patting one forearm.

"And I suspect he knows something I need to hear," Urma says.

"Something I need to say maybe, too. I'm not here to sell a painting," Roger says. "I may be new to this, Grandma, but I am not the only dead person in this room." He was always a charmer, smooth and quick, Urma thinks.

"Not quick enough," he says to Urma.

"Alright, you can read my thoughts, now, deceased Roger."

"Oh, you weren't talking out loud? Everyone here can hear them – your thoughts – you know."

*They can?* Urma thought.

*And you can hear us.* The painter sits on the north side of the table between Tom and Shannon. "I can only stay for a while. Please let me tell you my story." He turns to Kokum, who still has her arms crossed in disapproval. "I will then return to my travels. It may be this is part of my learning path." He grins at her, his white teeth gleaming. Kokum nods and he begins.

"Ever since I was a child I wanted to paint. You can see I wasn't horrible. Even sophisticated ladies like this one bought my work." He waves at the paintings, a delicate line drawing of a water bird, with a red moon, and an egret, bold among cattails.

Fox reaches across the table, hand outstretched. "I am honoured to meet the artist. My people also appreciated the flighted ones." He gestures at his tattooed chest.

"Very cool," the painter replies, seizing Fox's hand and pumping it sincerely.

Roger accepts a wine glass from Urma. "I painted," he says, "but I was also frightened by success. I remained poor, it seemed, while those who bought my work became wealthy. I could not feed my first girlfriend and my baby, so I left them. I miss my baby."

"I left my family too," Tom says. "It is not easy for a man to admit he cannot feed his children, that he is a burden to his wife." Tom rubs his hand beneath his nose. "It was the hardest thing I've ever done."

"We all miss our children. That's the down side about being dead." Shannon pulls a napkin from the table tight in her hands.

"Let him talk, so he can go, "Kokum instructs.

"Because I painted, I always had paint thinner handy, and soon I started using it to get high. It happens. I'm not proud of that. I started selling my paintings for solvent."

"But last time I saw you, you were straight, looked great, even had your baby daughter with you." A mere six months ago, Urma thinks.

"Seven. I was in the morgue for two weeks, while they tried to figure out what happened. But I'll tell you.

"So there was this party. A stupid party. One of those ones that may have started out as fun at first, lots of laughs, some talk, music and dancing, but after a few days, everyone was starting to get on each other's nerves.

"I was drinking, snorting, sniffing, you name it. Building a fog. Really out of it." Roger glances quickly at Urma, then Shannon. "Eileen was with me, sort of."

"Not a good place for her," Shannon murmurs, exchanging glances with Urma.

"So you may be one of the last people to have seen Eileen. Where were you?" Urma stands up.

"She was definitely the last person to see me alive." Roger shrugs. "Besides, your girlfriend shouldn't fool around right in front of you, right?"

"Girlfriend? She's just a kid, Roger! And your cousin!" Urma's hand curls into a fist.

"Fourth cousin by marriage, or something. We're all cousins." He looks at Shannon. "And there's only ten years between us. In some ways, lots of ways, she was more mature than me.

"Anyways, as I was saying, everyone was reaching the point of stupor. Everyone – there were only a few of us left. I was ready to crash out, but Eileen was still up, talking with this goofy kid. He was trying to hit on her, kept putting his hand on her breast. She kept telling him to fuck off, pushing him away. I don't know why she didn't just get up and walk away from him. Instead she kept trying to have this drunken discussion about some stupid zombie movie she thought he should see. Anyways, something about the way he kept pawing her and she kept pushing him away but letting him at the same time pissed me off, so I staggered over and yelled at him: *Get out of here.* I swiped an arm in his general direction.

"*What you saying, bro?*"

"*Get away from her.* I shoved him off the sofa. He jumped up from the floor and there was a knife in his hand. *Make me.* He slashed around like some kung fu hero."

The painter turns slowly to reveal the rend in his otherwise tidy checked shirt, and the bloody gash in his back. "No one I knew well, but still a cousin, right? And possessed by the bad spirits. He'll likely end up in a psych ward instead of a prison. At least I hope he does, because that's where he belongs. He really is a fool, poor kid. Anyways, I saw everything very clearly for a few seconds. So did Eileen. So did the kid."

Shannon grabs his wrists. "You brought my baby girl to a place like that?"

"I was there to protect her at first. She went to lots of parties. She kind of fell apart for a while after you died, Shannon."

"But that's not the way." Shannon glares at Roger, shakes his arms. "I know that's not the way to live."

"It is a way to die. Eileen was trying to be just like you, in her own way." Roger turns his arms so his hands enclose Shannon's.

"And you couldn't have stopped her," Dwain says to Roger.

"You could have been there for her!" Urma could feel her face age before them. "I should have been there for her. And for you, Roger." Urma focuses on her hands, clasped together now in a restless bundle. "So Eileen was dealing with her mother's death, your murder, and I was lying on my back in a downtown hospital bed."

"You didn't hold the bottle to her lips," Roger says. "She was running with a rough crowd, she was boozing heavily, and she didn't care what happened. Eileen was well on her way to being numb when I last saw her."

Shannon still grips Roger's wrist. Kokum intervenes.

"Let him go on his journey, Shannon. Let him go."

Shannon obeys, reluctantly.

"Such a waste." Urma shakes her head. "You were so talented, Roger."

"Like anyone else you know? I was wasting it. Someone else will have that talent now. That's how it works, you see. If you don't use your talent, you lose it. If you don't ask for help, you won't get any. And if you don't try, you stay stuck. Do you see, Urma?"

"Right, Roger. Thanks. I do see."

"Okay, I'm out of here. Love you, Kokum!" The painter reaches behind him and brings forward a bucket of fried chicken. "Here you go. I didn't have time to cook a thing, but enjoy. Most of you don't have cholesterol to worry about anymore. None for you, Urma. Or for the little ones." And he is gone.

"Little ones?"

## Memekwesowak

Shannon had introduced Urma to the little people, sort of, at the sun dance.

Urma did not stay for the entire sun dance, even though Shannon had asked her to be there, to be her support. On the last day, after Shannon and Eileen set out food in front of their tent, securing the tent from the kokocans, the negative spirits that whirl through the camp on the last morning, and then whirl through the dancers and their supporters, circle around the pole the wrong way, poke people with sticks, saying no when they mean yes, and laughing when they wanted to cry — the gunny-sack clowns — Urma was crowded out of her usual spot by the crush of new people arriving in time for the give-aways. Although Kokum tried to make her stay, signalling her to come sit with her close to the drummers, Urma knew it was time to go. Shannon was going to make it through the dancing. She only had a few hours left, and now there were lots of people there to wish her well if she collapsed. It was the same feeling Urma had when she went to see her family in Finland, her father's home country. She was welcome, but this was not home. Urma blessed the pole, as she had seen others do as they entered and left, thanked Kokum with a smile and appreciated, as she walked clockwise through the arbour and away from the circle, the strong feeling of community that was building as the ceremony was winding up to the feast.

Instead of attending the feast, Urma walked up the prairie trail on the side of the hill, to a spot where she hoped she could see a long way. In the bluff just before the perfect rise, she came across faded cloth tied to branches, and the remains of gifts — tiny toys, crumpled paper almost colourless, shiny stones and the remains of cigarettes – from a long-ago ceremony. Drawn to this place, she sat on a patch of grass and moss, and turned her head slowly from side to side. She was being watched. She could feel it. Nothing threatening. No kokocans, the contrary spirits that spill out of the hills. A presence as curious about her as she was about it. Quick. Not a deer. It would not have stayed. Not a big cat. Urma would not have stayed. Not a bear or coyote. Same thing. Maybe a badger. Something earthy. If she sat perfectly still, so did it. More than one, now. If she turned around suddenly, just the sound of the wind whipping through her hair, and they'd scatter. She reached carefully into her pocket and unwrapped a pink and white mint. She left it on top of its paper, with a cigarette she had been given at the sun dance. She felt eyes on her back as she walked back down the hill. Many days later, Kokum told her about the Memekwesowuk, the little people of the hills.

At Urma's dining room table, they are so shy, it is very hard to see them. Urma is glad she'd thought to put the metal utensils away. Kokum had said they are wary of metal. Was there something about jewellery too? Urma pulls off the only ring she wears, Shannon's ring – no, Eileen's ring – and puts it in her skirt pocket.

Gradually, Urma glimpses them. Their features fade when viewed directly, but through her peripheral vision, Urma could see the small quick fingers, reaching for a piece of bannock. Then the quizzical faces mopped with tangles of windswept hair, peering over the table edge. There are three of them, a formal delegation. They seem perfectly comfortable in the company of the dead. It is Urma they are skittish around.

"They know we can't hurt them, but for some reason living humans have a practise of capturing and studying things they don't understand," Fox explains.

"I would not do that to a guest in my house," Urma exclaims, overly loud. The little people scatter.

The guests at the table are silent for a few moments, and the tallest of the delegation reappears beside Kokum, and places a roll of bark with charcoal markings on the table.

> ### Wild Salad
> *1 handful of fresh, young Chicory leaves*
> *1 handful of fresh, young Dandelion leaves*
> *1 handful of Lamb's Quarter leaves*
> *1 handful of Shepherd's Purse leaves*
> *1 handful of Sheep Sorrel leaves*
> *1 handful of Mint leaves*
> *Leaves fresh (or dried) never wilted. (Poison when wilted.) Tear leaves into small pieces. Serve with crushed berries and vinegar or the cider from crushed bear berry and water left in the sun for two days.*

"You know, the Finns used to get along pretty good with these little ones," Tom says. "There are stories about marriages between the two. I'm sure you've heard them." Tom pours himself another shot of vodka and berry.

Urma nods. In fact, when she was little she used to imagine her father was part little people, he was so quick and strong and had such pointy ears. These folks don't have pointy ears, though. But as she is thinking about her father, the tallest of the three walks very cautiously towards her and gravely presents her with a set of sewn leaves, exquisitely lashed, full of a dizzying array of salad greens.

"Thank you," Urma says. "This looks wonderful."

"You can eat it, all of it, even the big leaf." His voice resonates with the rise and fall of an adolescent, sometimes deep, sometimes childish.

"These people are suffering the same kind of adjustments my people did, long ago." Fox touches the shoulder of the small man nearest him. "The weather is changing and they are suffering. Once farmers left milk or eggs or some small gift for them every day, but now there are so few farms that they've gone back to the wild, am I right?"

The smallest, a wee girl, nods at Fox. Her voice is so soft they have to stop moving dishes on the table to hear her. "It's the water. So much of it is bad. We have to travel long to find good water to drink."

"Don't I know it," Dwain says. "Our water supply is getting ruined, and no one seems to care. If I have one wish, it would be to make the people take care of their waters."

"If I could grant one wish," replies the middle-sized small one, a bit slyly, "that would be it."

"Where does that folk belief come from, that you little people can grant wishes?" Urma asks, and then, *And why am I bothering to speak out loud. Everyone but me can hear my thoughts.*

*You can hear ours too*, a voice mutters in her head, but she isn't sure who says it.

"We are very good at finding things that are lost, and at helping you lose things. Finding things has often been viewed as a form of magic, of granting a wish. Our tendency to pick up shiny things is not viewed with as much happiness." The tallest of the Memekwesowuk holds up the gold ring that

Urma had only moments before slipped into her pocket. "Are you missing anything else?"

"Yes." Urma slips the ring back on her finger and finds there are tears dripping down her cheeks. Shannon reaches over to pat Urma's hand and touch the ring where a sparkle of diamond flickers in the long light of evening. "I've lost Eileen. I'm so sorry, Shannon. I don't know where to find her."

Urma flings her head back and stares at the ceiling. This time the little people do not scatter. "How do I go about finding Eileen? She's sixteen and has a perfect right to be anywhere she wants to be. At least according to the police, to the social workers. Besides, who am I to her? We never did have a formalized arrangement for supervising her, for taking care of her, did we, Shannon? Just a friendship agreement. According to the authorities, she was old enough to have her own place, but she was never mature enough to maintain it." Urma drops her head again. She is getting one of her pounders, a headache that almost deafens her, the throbbing so loud in her ears. She turns to Shannon. "After you died, Eileen became more difficult, more distant, sunk into herself. She stopped talking to me, stopped coming by for meals, dropped out of school. I thought the school authorities would have been upset, but they were not.

"You know, I tried to report her as missing as well. The police seemed to be sympathetic, but there are so many missing girls. Before opening a missing persons file you have to look for the missing person yourself. I sent out emails, posted photographs, made phone calls. Hundreds of phone calls." Urma rubs her temples, and swipes at the tears swooping down her cheeks. "I knocked on doors, walked into bars and house parties, lots of places where I wasn't welcome, lots of places where Eileen could have been, but wasn't. I walked a different section of town every night. Weekends I went to other towns to look for her. No one knew where she was. No one would say where she was. I was okay with her not being with me, but I wanted to know she was safe, that she wasn't in some sort of pain.

"Then I got sick. I've been in my own damned fog for three months! And still no word from her. She must have thought I'd disappeared into thin air, and abandoned her. Shit! Excuse me." Urma leans behind the table, reaching for the tissue box on the side board. "Luckily, I still had a job waiting for me at the restaurant. I had to go back to work."

Back at the restaurant, Urma wasn't quite herself yet, shaky and fearful, and so very sad. One of the things that happen after any debilitating attack on the body, Urma guessed. Sadness, and fear. Fear of failure, of success, of sadness and happiness and loneliness and crowds.

After much agonizing and gnashing of teeth and cursing her lack of discipline – she had a missing person to find, after all – she had called upon her friend, the Princess.

The Princess was not a real princess. Urma met her on the neurological ward, where they were neighbours for ten days.

Urma's first words to her ward-mate were: "So what's with the exotic accent? You sound like a princess."

"Then for you, I shall be a princess." Princess lifted her left arm into the air above her bed, and waved a bejewelled hand over her face. "And then, for the purposes of our stay in this lovely establishment, you shall be a princess too."

"I'm not comfortable with that, Princess." Urma lifted herself on one elbow. "I'm Urma, with a 'u', which was probably a typographical error on my birth certificate, but 'ur' means something like earliest or primitive in some Germanic language, and that is more how I see myself. Besides, I'm a waitress, not someone who has ever been waited on."

"That is a pity." Princess lifted her head from her pillow to acknowledge Urma, who, she could see, was as unlike a princess as she was a waitress.

"I cannot imagine this – you do not belong in servant's black and white. You need to wear colours!"

"Not such a good idea in the neighbourhood where I work, Princess."

"I mean magnificent colours, not some blob of paisley in a gangster's handkerchief. I mean fuchsia and purple, fire and orange, emerald and lapis. These rags they want us to wear here are not acceptable. I'll have my son bring something for you. I have asked him to bring my silks. They are more feminine. These hospital gowns do not close properly. Besides, you should show a bit more décolletage."

"No, I really don't think –"

"Of course you may wear some of my rings and perhaps a pendant until your people bring in yours."

"I don't have any."

"But you should. Your fingers are perfect for flaunting stones."

"No people. My family is too far away, too scattered. And they have their own problems. I live alone."

"Ah, but no lover? Or perhaps you have many?"

"I'm very tired now, Princess. I'll try your rings on a bit later. Thanks." Urma slipped down into her pillow.

Princess spoke to the ceiling. "I heard you challenge the nurses. You are very strong to do that. They don't mean to be unreasonable, I don't think, but they must learn to not treat everyone like a cookie knife."

"Cutter."

"Yes. And when I heard you, I knew you were an ally."

"What are you in for, Princess?"

"Stroke. My right side. I walked a few steps today, but my foot has no feelings. I will have to relearn how to hold a fork, or a pen. How to write."

"You look perfectly well."

"So do you."

"Thanks, Princess."

Their alliance on the neurological ward turned into a powerful friendship in the three months since. They understood each other's injuries, the invisible hit. Others could see them out there functioning almost normally and think the illness was just a blip. Someone who has been through it knows better. There were support groups, therapeutic groups, assessment groups, physio groups, but Urma had to go back to work, and Princess chose not to attend, so they became each other's support.

After their stay in the ward, Urma would drop by to visit Princess on her days off. Princess had moved into assisted living. Urma was back in her tiny house, where her garden languished and spiders thrived, as it was all she could do to get to work and back every day. She slept without eating at home most days, so the pot luck was a huge output of energy. The weekly visits with Princess almost always involved meals out and the exchange of recipes, for Princess was a discerning gourmand, having maintained a healthy respect for European cuisine in her forty years in Canada.

Princess was also the best flower thief in the northern hemisphere, and loved nothing better than to help those in need, in her own way. Well, no, there are other things she liked to do better and did well: dress elegantly or outrageously, collect large semi-precious stones, preferably set so she could display them from her ears, her fingers or her neck, entertain an audience with her musical voice, collect bouquets of flowers (wild or tame, purchased or purloined), or seduce a potential lover. These are things Urma seldom thought about in her practical world. The colour and laughter the Princess brought to the ward and to Urma's life had speeded her way to better health.

What Princess knew about finding missing persons would fit on the head of a pin, but when it comes to losing things, she was world class, having lost something in almost every country in the western world. Keys, hats, jewellery, wallets, suitcases, portfolios, jackets, scarves, books, photographs, keepsakes and purchases had all been the subject of loss in her life, and of vigorous searches involving everyone in the vicinity. Princess, then, knew how to find people who know how to find things.

"St. Anthony is a personal acquaintance of mine," she said. "He is very busy, finding things for people, but I will intervene on your behalf. You must invite him to your dinner party."

"Pot luck."

"Very well, pot luck."

"Princess, would you like to join us?"

"I don't like such things so much. You always get too much of one thing and not enough another." Princess was not going out too much these days either, self-conscious of her limp, the fumbling hand, and her lopsided smile. "I'm not so interested in hanging out with the dead. I still have some living friends who amuse me. In any event, I'm not sure if St. Anthony will be able to eat just anything."

"Sure, being a saint and all. But he was human. I'll bet he'd go for some Thai food." Urma thumbed through her cookbooks and found these:

### Real Green Thai Curry
**For Green Paste**
*grind together with a little water*
*6–8 green chillies*
*3 spring onions, chopped along with the green*
*part (or 2 small button onions)*
*4 lemon grass leaves (optional)*
*2" piece ginger*
*3 tbsp. coriander leaves.*

**For Main Dish**
*1 chicken, about 700–800 gm, cut into pieces of*
*your choice*
*1 ½ cups coconut milk*
*1 ½ tsp. salt*
*a tiny piece of gur (jaggery or dark brown sugar)*
*1 tbsp. dhania powder (coriander)*
*1 tbsp. jeera powder*
*2 tbsp. oil.*

*Prepare the green paste by grinding everything together given under the green paste in the grinder.*
*Use little water if required for grinding. Grate one coconut. Soak in 1 ½ cups of warm water for 1-2 hours.*
*Churn in the mixer and strain to extract coconut milk.*

*In a dish add oil, green paste, coriander and jeera powder. Mix well.*
*Micro high uncovered 3 minutes. Add chicken. Mix well.*
*Micro high covered 4 minutes. Add salt, jaggery and coconut milk. Mix well so that jaggery dissolves. Let stand 2–3 minutes.*
*Serve garnished with chopped red chillies or coriander or basil leaves.*

*Note : This dish is supposed to be very hot. If a lesser hot dish is desired, reduce green chillies to 4–5. Instead of chicken, mixed vegetables can also be used.*

Or buy some green curry paste, and coconut milk, and cook them with vegetables, like Urma did. It is very hot too. Just in case, she also made this:

### Strawberry Chicken
*Sprinkle chicken with lime and cook in butter, add frozen strawberries when about half cooked. Pears are also good. When the chicken is cooked, remove the meat and fruit and add one cup of chicken stock to the liquid in the pan, bring to boil and stir in 1 tbsp cornstarch mixed with 2 tbsp. cold water. Simmer, salt and pepper and then pour sauce over chicken. Serve with rice – jasmine or basmati, but wild rice is just fine too.*

Even a saint couldn't resist such delicacies.

Urma has never had a saint over for a meal before, but when St. Anthony shows up, in a pair of clean, though slightly worn, blue jeans and a pristine white t-shirt, his shaggy hair tied with a strip of leather at his nape and sporting a neatly trimmed beard, she feels like she's known him for years. On his right chest, in plain black print his shirt reads "Seek and ye shall find."

"St. Anthony! Please join us!"

"Hey," he says, waving his hand in greeting all around. "Urma, my friend Princess called to say you needed help, but I think the only assistance you need tonight is help in eating all this food. I am so down for that. And here." He passes two elegant jugs to Urma. About one gallon each, they are glazed with a crane delicately stalking each side, the long neck forming the handle and spout respectively. "Some wine. Stop worrying about running out. These babies are bottomless. Just add water."

"Like the ones at the wedding in the biblical story?" Urma asks.

"They *are* the ones from the wedding. Drink up, folks."

"Well," Tom says, "I must try this one for sure, but you also need to taste my vodka and berries. Very special, too."

In the flurry for more glasses and drinks, and Kokum's tea (would she have a little bit of wine, since it is so special? Just a little bit, maybe) and Shannon's coffee (was she still pretending AA even now?) Anthony slips over to sit beside Urma. Her tear-filled eyes reflect the sunset, the darkening horizon, but she smiles at him. Dwain takes Shannon's hand in his, and they look at each other, then Urma, their eyes unreadable.

"Don't worry. I can help you with your loss."

"Oh, thank you, St. Anthony!" Urma hugs him. He smells like patchouli and lemon, reminding her of a boyfriend she had many years ago, when she was Eileen's age.

St. Anthony nods. "You will find everything you are looking for tonight, Urma. You know, by the time I was your age, I had sold all my possessions and already spent twenty years in a cave."

"What made you do that? Walk away from everything?"

"I really didn't walk away from everything. I was twenty and tired of materialism. Lots of people are at that age. I just stuck with it longer. And because of the prevailing social climate, it was considered a religious act, so I became the founder of Christian monasticism. I really am, or rather was, just a hermit. The rest of my story was given to me by Athanasius. St. Athanasius now, I understand." St. Anthony slings his arm lightly over Urma's shoulders. "Athanasius used to come by and hang out during my hermitage, interviewing me, taking notes. He tried the monastic life for a while, but he really was too much of a social animal. I guess you'd call him a journalist today. He did write my "Life." And lots of other important documents. So while he's remembered for his brain, I'm remembered as the saint of Domestic Animals and Finder of Lost Objects. Don't ask me why the domestic animals. I don't know. I lived most of my life in the Egyptian wilderness. There were wild animals, but domestic, not so much. But you see, Urma, I had not lost my memory, or my eyesight, or the use of my body. My mother and father were still alive when I returned home. I just happened to have good press which impressed the church fathers enough to make me into a saint." He grins and half-winks at Urma. "Now let's practise not talking. You just have to trust this, it's a bit of a trick, but with this crowd, believe me, if they don't hear you'll know."

"But how will I know who says what?"

Anthony is pouring wine and doesn't acknowledge her question.

"Oh, you'll know, alright."

"Okay, I don't know. Who said that?"

"You did," says Fox.

# LET THE FEAST BEGIN

Only one no-show, Urma thinks with relief.

"Everyone has arrived," Fox tells her in no uncertain terms.

"Everyone who is coming, I guess. Please, everyone, begin."

There is a moment's pause. Oh shit, Urma thinks. We have to have a grace. That's what you do with this many bosses in one room. Just, which one gets to do it? Urma's glance from face to face settles on Shannon's reassuring grin.

Of course, absolutely fearless Shannon. "Would you say a few words, my friend?"

No one could look more reverent on a moment's notice. Shannon bows her head, her straight glossy hair fringing her face in deep shade. "We around this table wish to thank the powers that be for allowing this very special gathering to occur. We thank each of our elders for blessing us with their presence. We thank Urma for inviting us into her home. We thank the creators for the riches of the earth before us. We will eat well and we are grateful. *Ekosi.* That is all I have to say. I have spoken. All my relations. Hey hey."

After the passing of platters, the clinking of plastic ware and the murmurs of appreciation, the conversation opens with the question of who might be the eldest of the elders at the table. St. Anthony looks like a clear winner in terms of longevity, having died at the ripe old age of one hundred and five, but the tallest of the little people clears his throat at that.

"I'm not sure if we measure time in the same manner as you, but I am considered young at one hundred and sixty winters, and as I am still alive, I may become even older, unlike each of you, with the notable exception of our hostess and her father. As you know, we can sometimes lose track of time, so many of our people are much older. We have no words for the amount of years passed in that way."

"You mean in the drumming hills?" Urma's mother and father had often told her variations on the legends of the little people, of humans following music into the hillsides, to reappear decades, even centuries later.

"Time is not necessarily as you see it, but yes, things do not happen in the same chronology with us. The passage of events is energy, not ticking clocks."

Urma blinks. The Memekwesowuk are alive, just from another measure of time. And St. Anthony seems very alive now. They all do. "Just a minute. Did you mention my father?"

St. Anthony nods to Urma, then continues. "I spent twenty years alone, and it could have been twenty minutes."

"I appear to be the eldest for plain old antiquity." Fox touches his right palm to his chest. "They say it was 500 B.C. when my body was buried in the bog. Your well-documented death, St. Anthony, was several hundred years later, in 356 A.D. You are also, are you not, the namesake for St. Anthony's Fire?"

"Most likely. I am saddened to be connected to a disease which has been the cause of so much human suffering. Fox, that was part of your death scene, right?"

"The worst part. Burning skin, dry gangrene, gastrointestinal symptoms I won't mention while we're eating. Is that how you passed on as well?"

"No, at my age, I just lay down one day and said that's enough. Letting go was the easiest thing in the world."

"That was the way I'd always hoped to go," Kokum says, and pauses to lick a bit of chicken from one finger. "But I was taken with a weak heart, and spent the last few weeks of my life unable to speak or walk or feed myself."

"I remember," Urma says. "I was just getting over Dwain and Shannon and then you go and die."

"That should never happen," Kokum says, catching Shannon's eye across the table. "A mother should never have to outlive her children."

"But the rest of us were there for you," Urma says.

"Yes, I tried to let go but you and my family were always around, keeping me there. Then one morning I was alone and strong enough to leave. It was a good thing for everyone."

"It's only human to want to keep your loved ones near you." Urma thinks of her own father, of his suffering.

From the other side of the table, Urma can hear Tom's low rumbling voice. He is conversing with a new arrival, a man hardly visible. Urma's foggy vision is playing tricks on her. This man is like smoke, like sunlight on dust motes. His features, when they are in focus, are the ice blue eyes and the slightly pointed ears of her father.

"*Joo, kylla, kitos,*" he is saying, *yes, well, thank you,* and then he smiles at Urma. "Well, hello Urma!"

"Dad."

"I'm sorry I'm late. I had some work to do. You have good company. I haven't seen this *poika* for a long time."

"Sixty years." Tom pats Father's shoulder.

"But Dad, you're not dead!"

"Not yet, daughter, but I wanted to be here. Besides, I haven't seen your house yet. You have done a good job of this. *Kaunis.*" He lifts a glass of Tom's *puolukka* and *rommi.* "*Kippis!*"

"Cheers, Dad." Urma lifts a glass. The entire table follows suit.

"Now. You've been taking care of me, of your mother, of others too. Good job." Father's voice wavers. "Time to take care of yourself too, Urma."

"Oh Dad, I love you! I'm so glad you can be here!" Before she can reach out across the table, or run around to be near him, her father fades away again. Her smile crumples. Of course he could not stay. If only he were out of his fog long enough to – to what? To protect her? To be there for her? To make everything else better?

"It is a flaw in the logic of human love that wants to keep loved ones in suffering." Kokum's bird-brown eyes glint. "Letting go is a higher love. There are worse things in life than being dead."

Urma's father was not dead, but she lost him fifteen years earlier, when a heart surgery took away his memory in huge swaths, leaving him child-like, with occasional clarity, and sometimes, with anger. Too much for Urma's mother to care for, and in fact a handful for any institution, he has been kept in the shadow land of chemical restraint ever since.

"I wish we would have just let him go out into a snow storm. I wish we'd been able to let him go with a drug overdose. We agreed not to intervene when his system stops working, but I wish he'd stayed healthy so I could still have my dad.

"Why did this happen to my father?" Urma asks Kokum.

Kokum reaches for her tea cup. "Do you think he chose this fog?"

"Yes, sometimes I do. There was too much change for him to accept, too many things he couldn't agree with, and too many years of not saying anything about these things, of pretending they weren't there, until they were not there."

"What things, my girl? We all have reasons to run away."

"Father was an immigrant, a farmer, a man who worked with his hands in the time of machines." Urma glances at Tom, then bites her bottom lip a moment. "And I guess mother wasn't easy."

"Mothers are never easy," Shannon says, tossing a slice of bannock towards Kokum. Kokum catches the bread, and attempts a stern glare.

"Your family members have their own lessons to learn, perhaps," Kokum says to Shannon, then turns to address Urma again. "Your job as the child is to learn from them, and perhaps not to repeat their mistakes."

Urma spoons green curry onto her plate, taking a moment to think. "So I should be grateful for my mother. From her mistakes I learned the importance of facing things head on, of clearing the clouds and looking, wide-eyed, into the jaws of whatever monster presents itself. Even though I prefer the fog. Wow, do I ever see where I learned that. I was born into a family of escape artists."

"And I left before I wanted to. You've got to wonder how that's fair." Dwain scoops out a perfectly set slice of lasagna for Shannon. "The guy I was working with ended up a cripple. People know, though, they know their time on earth is short. I did. I always knew."

"I didn't!" Shannon touches Dwain's cheek. "I always thought I'd go first. Such a coward I was, to hope to leave you with that pain, to not have to experience it myself."

Dwain took Shannon out for supper the Saturday before he died, her choice where, make it the best place in town, he said. As the sun set over the marina, enveloping their table on the deck in an orange glow, they held hands, sipped cola and gazed at each other.

Dwain fumbled in his pocket, and pulled out a cloth-covered box. "Shannon, here's something for you."

"For me? Oh thank you!" Shannon swung back the delicate hinge, revealing a thick gold ring, a sparkling embedded diamond. "Oh my god."

Dwain looked at the ring, then at Shannon. "If you don't like it we can look for another."

"No. The ring is perfect. It's just. Well. I'm not." Shannon closed the box.

Dwain reopened it quickly. "Here, just try it on." He slipped the ring on her left hand. "See. It even fits."

"But I don't. Dwain, this just isn't right. You know I'm not good for this." Shannon held her hand out. It did look pretty. No, elegant. No, as if it had always been there.

"Look, it's you. Please just wear it. I'm not going to pressure you to marry me, or anything, although I would. Just wear it, okay?"

Shannon flashed her dimpled smile. "Alright. It's the prettiest ring I've ever put on. Let's go somewhere to show it off."

They went out dancing and spent Sunday in bed, talking, caressing each other, having delicious sex.

Dwain drove back out to the pig farm Monday morning. The trench was still open, crumbly and the pipe was still kinked. The manager brought out a ladder. "If you're too scared I'm going down there."

"It's just not wise, but it's gotta be done." Dwain swung his legs over the sides first, so when the trench collapsed the manager was only part way down.

Half a ton of sodden clay flowed into Dwain's open mouth, his outstretched hands. His ears and nostrils were filled with mud. He stopped breathing before the shock of broken bones and crushed flesh sank in.

"A fast way to go." Dwain looks at Shannon. "Crushing is not pleasant. The other guy's legs got caught. He was there like that for a long time before we were found."

Shannon is twisting her napkin again. "You know, you know how that hit me. I lost my balance. Losing your love like that, after a lifetime of looking."

Not fair, Urma thinks, dipping into the strawberry sauce. "You left the rest of us too after that, Shannon. Your friends, your girl, your family."

Shannon ran past Urma, her breath ragged, flung herself in a booth at the back of the restaurant and buried her head in her arms. She was sobbing so hard she couldn't answer Urma's questions. "What's wrong, Shannon? What's happened? Has something happened to Eileen?"

"No. No. Dwain." She lifted her head. Streaks of mascara ran down her cheeks and smudged dark circles around her eyes, a ghastly clown, shuddering with anguish. "There was an accident. Oh god."

Urma left her to catch her breath, and to catch her own. Shit, why did such horrible things happen. She brought two coffees to the table. To hell with the rest of the customers. She was on a break. "Shannon, here's a coffee. Is he okay? Is Dwain okay?"

"Nooo!" She howled. The three other people in the place gathered their coats. No one wanted to be around pain. "No, he's died. He's been killed. He's dead."

"What happened, Shannon? Who told you this?"

"That guy he works with. They found him. Oh god."

"They found him?"

"The earth opened up and swallowed him. Just like he'd always been afraid of. Crushed. He was crushed and mangled and suffocated by earth. He had no chance. A wall of earth collapsed on him. He's gone." Shannon calmed down as she spoke, twisting the gold ring on her finger. She pulled it off and pushed it into Urma's hand. "Here, give this to Eileen when she's old enough. I can't stand to wear it right now. I never deserved to wear it."

"Of course you do. Don't talk crazy."

"I am crazy, right now. I'm going to get drunk."

"Which won't solve anything. Which won't bring him back."

"Nothing will bring him back. I just. I just don't want to feel anything for a while."

Shannon wiped her eyes with a paper napkin. "Do I look okay?"

"Hang out with me for a while," Urma suggested. "We can go for a movie or something. Let's pick up Eileen and go for pizza or a walk."

"Tell Eileen I love her bunches." That was the last time Urma saw Shannon outside of the hospital.

"And when I ended up in the care of doctors, they didn't know how to treat me," Shannon says.

"Mom's in the hospital. Come quick." Eileen's voice over the phone was breathless.

Urma signalled to the cook. "I'm off early," and half walked, half ran the mile to the hospital. Urma hated hospitals, hated emergency waiting rooms. Hated not knowing what was going on. Part of her wanted to run in any other direction.

Shannon was waiting for Monday. That was when the doctors could do the tests. Meanwhile, the pain buckled her entire body every few minutes, as if she were in labour, or electric shock therapy.

"Is there anything I can do for you?" Urma asked, trying not to look in panic, trying not to worry Eileen, who was already very worried.

"Stay with me."

So Urma tried to stay, taking shifts with Eileen, who would dash out for cokes and smokes, and dash back, breathless. And with Kokum, who sat by Shannon for the hour Eileen and Urma took to eat, holding Shannon's hand. When they returned, Shannon was sleeping for the first time, looking relaxed, relieved.

Kokum leaned over Shannon, parted her hair and pushed it from her forehead, kissing her there. "I don't think she will wake up again," she said to Eileen.

And she didn't wake up again.

Sometime in the middle of the night, Shannon half sat up, drew in a large breath and fell back, no longer breathing. Eileen looked across the bed at Urma, then placed Shannon's right hand over her chest.

"She didn't even say goodbye!" Eileen said in a garbled whisper. She stared at Urma, tearless, wide eyed.

"Wait here with your mother while I call Kokum," Urma said.

"No! Don't leave me here!"

"Do you want to call Kokum, then?"

"Kokum already said goodbye, didn't she. She knew Mom was going to die. I didn't get to say goodbye." Eileen shook her mother's shoulder. "I didn't get to say goodbye."

Urma came to her senses for a moment. They were in a hospital. Perhaps revival was a possibility. She pushed the red button.

"What are you doing?"

"Calling for help. A nurse or something."

"She's gone, Urma. You know that."

"Maybe they can bring her back."

"Not if she doesn't want to be brought back."

The medical system arrived and spun into action, but Eileen was right. Shannon's body was a chemical wasteland, and her blood was rejecting everything. It was the painkillers that did it, finally. She'd lost the methadone balance, and the medical system just helped her out the door.

"And you didn't care," Urma thinks.

"No, at the end I did care. I realized there was only one person I'd really let down, and it was too late to fix that," says Shannon. "I had failed to love myself."

"That is a woman's problem." Tom is buttering a healthy slice of bannock. "Women learn to love others early, but sometimes they forget to love themselves. It's not right, depending on a man for everything, even the love of yourself. No man, no matter how good, can do this."

"Tom, you thought women were out to get you. Blaming them for peeing in your wheat." Urma laughs.

Tom laughs louder. "One winter," he says, " I wake up and realize I could fail. I have to find someone to blame. I could feel the need of the woman I left. Maybe she was cursing me.

Maybe I was cursing myself. I had a dream of coming back into my family like an old time hero, but like the Finn heroes of old, I was a fool, tricked by my own stubborn pride."

It was true. Vainamoinen, the singer in the Finnish myths, was foiled by the Maid of the North time and time again. At one point she had both the sun and the moon in storage while the heroes of old conspired to woo her daughter. The daughter dropped her suitors, one by one, from her sleigh, laughing. The heroes of old laughed at themselves too, and went back to work – the sun and moon were freed in the end.

"The heroes had big ideas. Me too. But big ideas are not enough to eat. Big ideas can only feed the heart for so long." Tom drains his glass.

"Little ideas don't feed the heart at all," Shannon says. "If I'd been braver, if I'd been stronger, I would have had my girl with me."

"At least you guys had some ideas. Some dreams." Urma focuses on her hands, clasped on her lap. "After I find Eileen, I have nothing to live for."

There was a silence. Urma senses that all eyes are on her.

"Afraid of success," Shannon half-whispers.

"Don't be so hard on yourselves." Kokum waves a finger. "You did the best you could. Loss can make you stronger, too, you know. We have a choice, all of us. I myself lost three children, and their memory stays with me always. There was nothing I could do, though. Their time had come, and their path was not with me. Shannon, you were lucky to have your girl with you as long as you did. I lost your grandparents when I was much younger.

"One day an Indian agent came through the settlement and took all the children." Kokum settles, ready to tell her story.

"Some families tried to hide their kids, and some children ran away, but most of us were lost to the residential school. You all know the stories – we couldn't speak our own language, practise our own ceremonies, wear our own clothing. Our hair was shaved off, and we were at the mercy of strangers who viewed us as less than human. That's what people say.

"Maybe I was lucky. The nuns were very nice to me. They taught me how to cook their style of food and how to be very clean. Everything was always boiled and bleached, and the food was plain but healthy. I missed good meat, and I missed my family, and I missed being free in the village, but I think my parents suffered more. Whenever I went home, they were surprised at my strangeness, and I think that, more than my absence, hurt their hearts.

"We forgot how to take care of our children in that generation. We forgot how to take care of our elderly in the next. Something broke there. Once there was no need to look for love. We lived in it. Now we are alone, and unless we are very strong, we become closed, afraid of more pain. Being open to love is the greatest act of bravery there is, the biggest idea there is."

"More important than life or death, Kokum?" Urma is circling the table, wine jug in her left hand, tea pot in her right.

"Because it does not die. Yes."

"Exactly!" Shannon says. "Like, I never did give up on Eileen, not really. Social Services took Eileen away three times, and then once and for all, but I kept in touch with my girl. I followed her from foster home to foster home."

"But were the social workers wrong, Shannon?" Urma had witnessed Shannon's frustrations with the system more than once.

"The workers are damned if they do and damned if they don't. How can you tell if a child is in danger? Eileen ran away from the foster homes, but she was too young to live on the street, too afraid to come home. I was failing her. Badly." Shannon unfolds the linen napkin, smoothes out the crumpled surface against her thigh.

"Life in care was not the answer. Those foster mothers admit it is a business, that they deliberately do not get too attached to the kids. Kids come and go and it's their job to provide a safe place, nothing more. Sometimes it's quite a bit less." Shannon pauses long enough to nibble on a corner of bannock. She does not look up, and the pot luck guests wait quietly as she gathers her thoughts.

"The worker told me and my girl that 'mom is bad for you right now, and you will be better off without her for a while'. Workers have a habit, or maybe it's part of their training, of talking about you as if you aren't in the room and part of the conversation. Dehumanizing, but it makes the next step easier. What my girl heard was 'mom is bad' and she remembers that." Shannon raises her head, her eyes gleaming, and smiles at Kokum and then at Urma.

"Never mind. I never gave up on my daughter. I think Eileen grew up knowing love."

"Do you think my kid will ever be able to trust anyone enough?" Shannon had asked Urma one night. They'd just been to a movie, something Urma almost never did. It was Shannon's pick, a scary one. The alien monster alarmed Urma; her arm flew up, hit the popcorn into the air all around them, and caused the women to giggle through the most frightening scene, much to the irritation of the other viewers.

"Not if you take her to movies like that one," Urma joked. "I'm going to have nightmares." Urma unlocked the car doors and slung herself behind the wheel.

The new worker had arranged a visit with Eileen and Shannon and it had gone well, according to Shannon. Eileen would be old enough to choose where she wanted to stay in a couple of months, and she was, as often as not, with her mother again these days anyway, although in theory the worker and the foster home did not know.

"I want her to know there are good people in the world for her." Shannon settled into the passenger seat and pulled down the visor to check her makeup.

"Just be there, and it will be okay. Okay?" Urma had told her.

"But I'm not there for her now," Shannon says, leaning over Urma's dining room table to scoop up the last of the strawberry chicken. "I know you will find her, Urma."

"But what if I'm not able to. What if I don't know what to do when I do find her?"

"Urma," Kokum commands, "you do what women always do, what always allows the wheel to continue to turn. You clean up, tidy up, and when everything is sorted, you follow your heart."

"Follow your heart. What does that mean?"

"It means opening up, discovering your dreams, revealing yourself to someone else."

"And how will that help Eileen?" Urma asks.

"Maybe this isn't about Eileen." Shannon says it, but Urma can tell everyone else is thinking it.

"So Urma, what questions are not answered for you tonight?" Fox Man's eye teeth glisten.

"At least one. I still don't know where I can find Eileen."

"You really are blind, aren't you?" Tom waves a scolding finger at her.

"What? What?"

St. Anthony catches Urma's hand. "You can accept everyone's death here. What if she is, too? Another missing woman. Another teenager lost. Another urban kid gone."

"She is just a kid. I have to know." Urma pulls her hand away to tap it, a small fist, on the table top.

Everyone is looking at her now. "Know what? Details?" asks St. Anthony.

"Where I can find her. How much she suffered." Urma blushes. "No, is there anything I can do to prevent her suffering?"

"No," says Shannon. "There is really nothing you can do to prevent the suffering of others. You have to do that for yourself."

"The real mystery here, Urma, as I see it, is how are you going to die?" Kokum pats her lips with a napkin. "This was all very good."

Urma shakes her head. Her fluttering hair causes the little ones to take a half step back. "I don't want to know that."

"Of course you do. You want to know," says Dwain, "but here's the bad news. We can't tell you. It hasn't happened yet. You do have choices."

"Thank goodness for that."

"But we can predict what is likely." Fox looks around the room.

"The way we see it." Tom nods at Fox.

"Don't bother. Please." Urma begins stacking the empty plates near her.

"Yes. You called us. We didn't call you," Shannon says.

Urma stands and begins clearing dishes from the table. "I think it's time for dessert."

St. Anthony puts his arm over Urma's shoulder, gently guiding her back to her chair. "I think it's time for you."

Urma sits on the edge of her chair, her eyes flicking from one face to the next around the table. She takes a deep breath. "Okay, shoot. No, don't shoot." Her nervous laugh breaks into a hiccough.

"Here are the possibilities." Fox begins, ticking them off on his fingers. "A quick bleed; a zombie life state; or a long and healthy life."

"Right," Urma says. "I knew that."

"Smile." Shannon smiles. "Hey, it's not like you have cancer or something."

Tom nods. "Your dreams will be your strength. Find them."

Dwain clears his throat. "Everyone is a potential undead."

"And we don't mean zombie as in rotting flesh," says St. Anthony, "although that happens too." He glances at Shannon. "We mean zombie as in rotting brain. Work on that. You don't want to go there. Your dad doesn't want you to go there."

"You guys, stop picking on me," Urma cries. "Stop!"

"So, follow your heart." Shannon waves her napkin like a flag.

Kokum shakes a gnarled finger at Urma. "Be a warrior."

"It hurts sometimes," says Dwain.

"And you may make mistakes," Tom adds.

"Lots of mistakes." Shannon grins.

"But that's not the hard part." Fox reaches for his goblet of wine.

"Moving forward is always easier than standing still." St. Anthony pats Urma's back. "Which is what you're doing right now."

"Standing still? Not entirely." Urma rubs her forehead. "I mean, it's tough when I'm not totally with it. When I forget things, deliberately don't see things." Urma looks around the table. "So, you really don't accept excuses here, do you? Okay, in my defence, I've been through a lot. You have put me through a lot, Shannon.

"God, my head hurts." Urma kneads the back of her skull, then grins at Shannon. "But there is some light on the horizon, I guess. A flicker. There's this guy I just met. He's a doctor and I'm not sure –"

Shannon shrieks. "You're in love! Urma's in love! I'm so happy for you!"

"Thank you, my friend. I'm not sure if –"

"It will be perfect. Listen, I will want to know everything!"

"But about Eileen –"

"She's beyond your help, my girl," Kokum says. "Move forward. Imagine something good for yourself."

"Like dessert?" Urma leans over to the sideboard, and lifts a stack of fresh plates to the table. She starts by passing Shannon a dessert-plate full of crab apple crisp. "Here, here's what I've learned from you. Try some of the bittersweet Finnish sauce on top. You believed in love after everyone else in your life failed you."

"Maybe that's why I believed. I had to. Maybe it's not possible to know the value of love before loss of some sort."

But the other options are to close off, Urma thinks, to call it all a game, to call that thing that happens between people a romantic illusion, or an unhealthy dependency or an obsession, or –

"An addiction. That's what you thought when I was alive. Just another addiction."

"And I was wrong. I'm sorry." Urma serves herself some puolukka berries.

"No, you weren't totally wrong. I was all over the map. God, when I met you I thought everybody had an angle."

That was true. There were a few awkward moments at the beginning of their friendship. "I thought you were trying to mark me," Urma agrees.

"I was. You had to be in it for sex or money or drugs or something. Friendship didn't even occur to me." Shannon grins at Urma. "You wanted to just hang out? That was a new one."

"It was the poetry, Shannon. Or maybe I was a wanna-be? Or a cultural voyeur? Or a street level voyeur?" Urma waves her plastic fork in a circle. "At some point I was all of those."

Kokum clears her throat. "Many people come to the Cree nation looking for romance and for spiritual power. I watched you at the sun dance, Urma. You wanted to learn, yes, but you were giving energy, not taking away. Not just looking."

Urma's eyes gleam in the darkening room. "Oh, Kokum, I wanted to be part of that ceremony and that community so much. Such a beautiful thing. But I know even if I changed my entire life, which I am not willing to do, I could not ever really fit in. It was an honour to have the illusion of belonging, even for that day."

"*Sisu!*" Tom exclaims. "Stubborn pride. Independent to the end. Do you ever wonder why the Finns live in the valleys, the rocky hillsides, by the northern lakes? It is easier to be alone with yourself there." Tom stands up. "Don't be afraid to be alone, *tytta*. And now I will go." Tom's cheek bones push his eye corners into a signature Finnish squint as he smiles at her.

"I'm not, now. Not afraid, and not alone. Thank you, Tom, for being here." Urma stands to shake his hand but he is already gone.

"We have something to tell you, living human," the tallest of the little people says. "About being alone. We found one of your children, out in the valley. She was lost or left there to die. There are worse places than under the open sky, but she was –"

"Worried," the tiny woman continues. "She said *No one will ever find me. I have disappeared.* She was too weak to move, but we kept the meat eaters away until she was bones again.

"We carried her bones to a hillside, beside the rocks. We thought her people might like to know."

"How old was she? How big?" Urma's voice breaks. "Could she have been Eileen? Looks like Shannon, hair like mine? About this tall?"

All three of them shrug. "She was lying down. It was not long ago. Within the last five full moons. Winter hasn't fallen on her bones."

Oh god, Urma thinks. What will I do with this? How many little girls have gone missing recently? Perhaps she's not Eileen. Urma will need to call the police, and what will she say? I was given a hot tip by three leprechauns who happened to be at my house for a pot luck?

"That is the best we can do. The hill is that way," the shortest one says, pointing east with her bottom lip. "Not far. Less than a day's travel. You will know it."

"I will help you." St. Anthony smiles at Urma. "Go for a walk in the hills."

"We have eaten well." The little people stand away from the table as one, and then are gone.

Urma realizes she hadn't even asked their names.

"What you do in the privacy of your own home is written in the streets of your city. What you think in your most private thoughts is written in big letters in the sky." Fox drains the last of his wine. "They called Tom catatonic when they stripped him of his dream. St. Anthony spent twenty years in a cave. I arranged for my own death."

"There's nothing sensible about a guy climbing into a channel he knows is going to collapse," Dwain says.

"Or drugging yourself to death," Shannon says, and presses her lips together.

"We have all been called crazy at one time or another." Fox stands, straightens his vest, and smiles, showing his elegant eye teeth once more. "You will find people who understand."

"Sure, maybe I'm crazy, choosing to spend time with the dead." Urma struggles to find a word to include everyone. "With the inter-dimensional." She stands, takes a few steps towards Fox, holding out her hand.

Fox takes her hand in both of his. "Thank you for inviting me to this most auspicious gathering. It has been a great honour to share this time with you. Do go for that walk in the hills. Find some rest for that little girl."

"I will look for her. I'm resisting the idea. I'm afraid of what I may find, or that I may not find anything. Afraid of success and afraid of failure."

"Remember, you are not alone." Fox smiles, his eye teeth glinting. "Despite what Tom says. Adieu."

"It is good you will not be alone on this earth, too." Kokum shakes the crumbs from her skirt.

"Kokum. Thank you for joining us. I miss your wisdom so much."

"Thank you for the good meal. The chicken was very good. You do not need to miss me. I have this for you." She passes Urma a fresh braid of sweetgrass. "Burn it and think of me. Maybe sometimes you will even listen to what you're told."

"Yes Kokum. Love you!" Urma watches Kokum float gracefully into the west.

"Your Kokum is a very wise woman, Urma." St. Anthony rises from the table. "You've received very good advice tonight. Check it out."

Urma takes in a deep breath. "OK. Thanks, St. Anthony."

"Thank you. This was great." He throws one arm around Urma, and squeezes her shoulders. "I can always count on the Princess to call me in for an interesting time."

"Why is it, then, that some people tend to lose things more than others?"

"That is a long story for another time, Urma. Even saints get tired. See you." His white shirt becomes a star in the new night sky.

"See you later! In the hills! Oh shoot, do you think he'll forget?"

Dwain looks at Shannon meaningfully. "Well, I guess it's time for me to go too. But here's a news flash for you, Urma. Love does not die. It just gets bigger and better, deeper and more complex. I mean, I'm glad for you that you are open to love again."

"Thanks for that, Dwain. Shannon? I really don't want you to go."

"I know. I've got to. You're alright now, aren't you?" Shannon reaches over to push a strand of hair from Urma's face. "Of course you are. You're looking for love."

"In all the wrong places, I know. I know the song." Urma wraps her arms around Dwain and then around Shannon, and pushes back, her eyes wet. "But I have dishes to do. Yes, I'm fine. I'm so glad to see you again. Love you, my friend." Urma watches Shannon and Dwain disappear, hand in hand.

"Bye, Urma. Much love!"

"Shannon! What am I supposed to do with your poetry? Damn!"

Urma turns to the table. There is a lot to clear. She has used every glass and cup in the house. She picks up the two wine jugs and carries them carefully to the kitchen counter.

Urma calls the Princess, and describes the evening's guests. "And you missed an excellent dinner, Princess. I'll save you some of the leftovers. The wine was particularly good. Brought by St. Anthony. I hope he can help me find Eileen."

"Oh really," Princess says. "You doubt St. Anthony? How dare you! Now the lost is found."

"Not quite," Urma admits. "What are you doing next weekend? Will you come with me for a walk in the hills?"

"I am not interested in that much wild nature. Maybe you could ask that nice doctor to join you."

Urma nods to the telephone receiver. She has a hunch he'd be a good person to have there, that he would understand. "Being a professional, he would know what to do with whatever it is I find out there." Urma imagines the two of them standing over the bones, the broken body of the girl who could be Eileen.

"Remember, you have already St. Anthony guiding you. And these little minnie-what-it-is. Is it possible with a stranger you might scare her away?"

Again, Urma nods. Princess knows about finding things, and perhaps people. In the end, Urma walks into the hills alone.

She drives east, as the Memekwesowak instructed. After half an hour or so, at about the time she has decided this is craziness, she comes out of the flats and into the badlands. On the highest hill, three erratics lean together like a European stone circle.

"There," Urma hears, as she presses her foot on the brakes.

The wind whistles through her hair, her ears thudding with the effort of the climb through the ripening prairie grasses. Her car, leaning slightly over the ditch side, glints like a colourful toy below. In the ravines, chokecherries hang like grapes. She will pick some on the way down. Urma smiles. The bitter berries remind her of Tom's *puolukka*, of Shannon's crab apples. Of the red wine Fox enjoyed so much. Urma carries a bottle of St. Anthony's wine slung over her shoulder. Nearer the rock circle the grasses thin, drying in the fine earth, and mounds of cactus cling to the hillside. Urma pauses to catch her breath, and picks one of the late cactus fruit. Kokum showed her how to eat these prairie delicacies many years ago. The juice is sweet, like kiwi. Urma picks a couple more and leans into the hill for the last dozen feet.

Around the stones, a path of hard packed earth has formed. Urma follows the circle around the nearest promontory, turning into the shelter between, almost tripping on Eileen in the process.

Eileen crouches in the shade beneath the jagged edges of the stones, glancing up as Urma pauses above her. She rises and Urma pulls her into a bear hug.

"I've been looking for you everywhere, Eileen. What the hell are you doing here?"

"Hey, Urma. It's good to see you. This is just where I ended up."

"Oh." Urma lets herself fall onto the earth by a neat pile of human bones. She shudders, looking from the girl's face to her earthly remains, and back to Eileen. Tears begin to stream down her cheeks. "So I guess it's a good thing I came up here."

Eileen settles herself, comfortably cross legged, facing Urma. "I was hoping someone would find me."

"You understand how desperate I was to find you? You understand that I've been hanging around with dead people and spirits and little people, and I must be crazy! And why do I have to go hill-climbing and practically give myself another brain haemorrhage to find you? I invited you, and everyone else came to me. Your Mom was there, damn it!" Urma leans over, shakes Eileen's thin shoulder.

"They're all dead!" Eileen shudders.

"Eileen! So are you. Dead." Urma clenches and unclenches a fist, and finally brings her hand just above her eye sockets, rubbing her knuckle to her forehead. "Why didn't you join us?"

Eileen stretches slowly, yawning a bit, the way people do when they need oxygen. "I guess I was afraid."

"Yeah, well hiding up here in the middle of nowhere kind of gave that away. Afraid of what?" Urma cups a hand to Eileen's chin. "And you, afraid?"

"Okay, Kokum says there's this journey I'm supposed to be taking," Eileen says.

"Yeah, you're to visit all the directions and learn the lessons you missed on earth."

"Well, I haven't started my homework yet."

Urma stares at her young friend, but neither of them can hold it back: they start to laugh. Urma's laughter turns into hiccoughing sobs. "What the hell, Eileen."

Eileen pulls Urma's fist open, where the cactus fruit is cradled and unbruised. Her naturally sullen features give way to a huge grin. "Since I missed the feast, how about some fruit?"

"All yours, girl."

"Man, this is great. I love wild stuff."

"You always did."

*I can hear your thoughts too, you know,* Eileen thinks.

*Then you know I'm not going to let you get away without telling me what's up with hiding. And disappearing.*

*Then I know you're still mad at me. Can I have some wine?*

*I guess a bit won't hurt. Of course I'm still mad at you.* Urma undoes the canteen and lifts it up in salute before taking a mouthful herself.

*Then I'm sorry, alright?* Eileen takes the bottle.

*All right.*

*All right then.* Eileen takes a sip of the sweet blood-like wine.

Ten seconds with Eileen and Urma is arguing like a sixteen year old too. "So here's why I'm mad. You left in a really bad way. Really bad, Eileen. You were bright and independent and –"

"Scared. And really, really depressed."

"So, okay, I need to know. Why – how did you die?"

"I already told you I'd go with a beer in one hand and a cigarette in the other. Just like Janis."

It was the dog days of August, during the summer after Shannon had died, and about the time going back to school seemed like not such a bad idea. Urma leaned behind the counter of the café, in front of the whirring fan, when Eileen sauntered in.

"Hey, good to see you. How's it going?" Urma reached for a tall, frosted glass. "The usual?"

Eileen nodded and straddled one of the plastic-topped twirling stools at the counter. "Boring as usual. How's your summer?" Everything was boring to Eileen. She was one of those people who could read a book in about an hour and remember all the nuances of the plot, walk into a room and immediately memorize every detail of the contents. She always seemed to know more than a kid should.

"Working. Nothing new?" Urma placed an icy cola on the counter. "Where are you staying these days?"

"At a friend's." Couch surfing was the street term. "It's all good." Eileen's eyes did that little sliding thing, so much like her mother. "I wouldn't just disappear on you, you know."

"Better not. I promised your mom I'd keep an eye on you."

"Yeah, well, she disappeared. Lots of times."

"Well, you don't need to," Urma said. "You know, your mom and I, we did pretty good for our age, growing up with all the good folks dying around us."

"Such as?"

"Such as Janis and Jimmi, Morrison and JFK and King. No one expected to live long. Not really."

"Well, if I go, I'll go like Janis, with a beer in one hand and a cigarette in the other."

"I remember you saying that," Urma says. "I just never suspected you'd be goofy enough to do it."

"It was easy. I was out in the country, at the grad party, and I left it. It was such bullshit. I just walked away, down this dirt road. I was half cut, saw a pair of headlights, and said, why not? So I jumped. The driver didn't even slow down, likely drunk himself. Likely thought he hit a deer." Eileen paused to lift the canteen once more. She cleared her throat.

"The hit didn't quite kill me, but the impact threw me quite a ways off the road. When I opened my eyes it was morning and I was really mixed up, you know? And my head hurt, and I couldn't walk right and I felt weird, like it was really cold, like I was freezing to death and I started thinking I was going to die of hypothermia like those guys the cops take on starlight tours, but it wasn't really that cold. I was just really messed up. And I stumbled around for a while and I found this spot under a poplar tree, by this slough. It smelled so good, like new life, like spring, and I fell asleep there." Eileen pauses to savour the wine.

"And didn't wake up?" asks Urma, taking the bottle from Eileen.

"No, I was awake and asleep for a while but too mangled to move. It hurt, but if I just went with it, the pain was not as much as I'd imagined it would be. Likely not as painful as your headaches, Urma. I was worried that you would worry, but I was ready to rest. Could I have a bit more?"

"I guess. What harm could it do?" Urma lifts the canteen to her own lips, then passes it back. "But why?"

"Like I said. Okay, so it wasn't the brightest thing to do."

"Damned selfish." Urma moves her legs to a more comfortable position, avoiding the bones. Eileen's skull is grinning at her. Urma turns back to the girl seated across from her in this rocky shelter.

"But it did get my name on the big screen."

"If you call Child Find the big screen." Urma's tears spill down her cheeks. She digs into her jeans pocket, pulling out a tissue. "You should have stuck it out. You could have done better."

"Okay, so I already said it was a stupid thing to do."

"Okay. But I'm still mad about it." Urma blows her nose hard.

"Okay," Eileen says, passing Urma the wine.

"So I'm glad to see you. I really missed you," Urma admits.

"Hey, sorry for all the worry. Didn't you get my message?"

"What message, Eileen?"

"When I died, I came to visit you and tried to do that *impress a message* thing. It's not as easy as it sounds."

Urma half laughs and shakes her head. "It was the not knowing – you could have been in real trouble, sick or in pain, or lost and not able to call home. Shit, you were in real trouble, in pain, lost." Urma wipes tears from her face.

"Yeah. I didn't want to be here anymore. I didn't know what I wanted, and didn't want what I knew. You know? And then Mom died. And Kokum. And Roger. But I'll never do something like that again."

"No kidding."

"You were really messed, huh?"

"I damn near died with worry. And grief."

Eileen puts a hand on Urma's arm. "Everyone dies, Urma."

"That's true, of course. Everyone dies. You know what else is true, Eileen?"

"What?"

"You still have homework to do." Urma points to the sky. "I have a feeling there are some people waiting to help you. I'm not sure if I should be touching this after drinking St. Anthony's wine." Urma pulls a braid of sweetgrass from her pack sack. "It's not proper protocol, but it feels alright."

"Kokum will let me know, I'm sure. So what are we waiting for?" Eileen stands and stretches.

Amongst the standing stones, orange, red, and ochre with lichen, in the simple shelter where the bones of Eileen rest, in that small calm place, Urma lights the sweetgrass. The smoke of the smudge forms a ring of faces. They seem to be smiling. Eileen reaches out for them. Urma touches her arm, as if to hold her back. She pulls Shannon's ring from her finger. "Here, you may need this, Eileen."

"I need nothing," Eileen smiles. "See you later, Urma."

Urma drops the small gold circle among the bones, faces the skull, and grins.

# Acknowledgements

Thanks to all the writers who inspired me in the many rewrites of this novella. I have benefited from the wisdom of Byrna Barclay, Linda Biasotto, Annette Bower, Bob Currie, Ibi Kaslik (thanks for the zombies!), Barbara Kahan, Robert Kroetsch (who recognized the quest), Jackie Lay, Dave Margoshes, Kim Morrissey, Colleen Murphy (who midwifed the mystery), Pat Krause, and James Trettwer. I love you guys.

Thank you, John Calabro, for a fine final edit.

Thank you to Cliff Dubois, a talented artist as well, for permission to use the artwork of Christopher Stanley Dubois.

This book is dedicated with much love to the memory of Stanley Dubois, Marlyn Obey, Agnes Carriere, Audrey Prentice, and my father, Ilmeri Onni Niskala.

And a big bouquet to Lala Heine Koehn for introducing me to St. Anthony.